Their Evil Ways

Solo whist. Less than 50p in the pot and Sammy had made a bad call. It hadn't been a World Championship. Nobody was going to retire to some tax haven with 50p.

But Sammy's partner had a temper and the smack in the mouth he gave Sammy happened to prove lethal. So Solly Daniels had a corpse on his hands, and neither he nor the other two players were going to tell the police. The police would think Sammy had been murdered, and at best there'd be big trouble.

An attempt to dispose of the corpse ends in a grotesque fiasco in a cemetery. This brings the police on the scene, complete with their very logical belief that their man had been murdered.

Here also is portrayed the squalor of the North End Division of the northern city of Lessford, which has featured in many of John Wainwright's earlier novels: a Hogarthian evocation of criminality, greed, stupidity, lust, despair. In this jungle there are police forces on the prowl, some of whose members are not much better than the scum they deal with, others of power and integrity. A formidable character — Detective Chief Superintendent Flensing — joins the array of dominating police officers who have featured in John Wainwright's novels.

As always, the plot is intricate with many strands. Starting with an accident that looks like a murder it builds up to such pressure — uncovers so much dirt — that a real murder is committed. There are many surprises . . . and once again this most prolific and gifted teller of stories about crime invents a tale that grips and holds.

THEIR EVIL WAYS

John Wainwright

Macmillan London

ISBN 0 333 34620 3

First published 1983 by
MACMILLAN LONDON LIMITED
London and Basingstoke
Associated companies in Auckland, Dallas, Delhi,
Dublin, Hong Kong, Johannesburg, Lagos, Manzini,
Melbourne, Nairobi, New York, Singapore, Tokyo,
Washington and Zaria

Typeset by
MESSENGERTYPE
Chatham, Kent

Printed in Great Britain by
THE ANCHOR PRESS LIMITED
Tiptree, Essex

Bound in Great Britain by
WM. BRENDON AND SON LIMITED
Tiptree, Essex

ONE

It was a nice night. Unseasonal, in that it was uncommonly *seasonal*; Monday, December 14th, a mere nine shopping days to Christmas, and already the snow and ice had arrived with the obvious intention of making this particular Yuletide deep and crisp and even in true Dickensian tradition. Groups of kids trudged the pavements, stopped at doors, gathered themselves into a tiny phalanx the better to penetrate the woodwork with unmelodious noise, bawled the first chorus of *Good King Wenceslas* then hammered the door in youthful expectation. At one house, an irate male voice answered the knock with, 'I'll have the bloody dog on you, if I open that door.'

It was a sentiment Police Constable Adamson could understand.

Snow (in the considered opinion of P.C. Adamson) was great stuff on Christmas cards. Off Christmas cards, you could keep it. Every last geometrically perfect shape. It didn't even look nice. By the time the local council workers had ploughed it, gritted it, shoved it into untidy heaps along the sides of the streets; by the time the general muck had seeped into and stained it, it looked as picturesque as the overspill from a sewage-farm. It was cold, it was wet, it was sloshy and, come a couple of hours from now, it would be dangerous. Night after night it froze. Solid! The thin film of surface water where pedestrians had stamped the snow solid, became as treacherous as moist glass to walk on. The mounds at the kerb edge could crack an ankle, break a leg, without even trying. Snow? Stuff snow. If he never saw snow again, he'd die a happy man.

At the moment he was *not* a happy man. He was cold, he was miserable and he was disgusted. Disgusted that a prize nerk, like Detective Sergeant Ballester, should carry the power and authority to make a hard-working copper stand around in brass-monkey weather watching sod-all. Nor could it be argued that Adamson had not pointed out to D.S. Ballester the error of his judgement.

9

'He's a nothing, sarge. A pint-sized loudmouth. He hasn't the guts to break into his own gas meter.'

'I have it on good authority.'

'Somebody's having you on.'

'*Very* good authority.'

'Sergeant, I *know* the snivelling little bugger. He'd run a mile. Believe me, you wouldn't see his arse for dust.'

'A job, constable. A night job. A *big* job. Other than that, I haven't any details. Just that Cutter's in on it.'

'Cutter!'

'I want him watched. Every night, from the time he gets home from work . . .'

'He doesn't work.'

'. . . until you're sure he's gone to bed. Until you're *certain*.'

And that was it. Some smart-talking creep had conned a couple of pints, maybe a couple of quid, from a dozy bloody detective sergeant and he (Police Constable Peter Adamson) had been lumbered with "observation duty" upon the hovel Tim "Titch" Cutter called home. Forever and ever amen, too. Because, as sure as God made green apples, Ballester wouldn't call it off in the foreseeable future. Ballester wasn't the sort of guy to admit to having been taken for a ta-ta too readily. The small matter of a fifty-year-old copper having his balls frozen off as a nightly performance didn't add up to a spit in the wind. Ballester was right, because Ballester was *always* right. He was that brand of idiot.

Adamson stamped his feet, but carefully because the snow was building up under the soles of his boots and any serious attempt at callisthenics would have shot his feet from under him and probably broken his neck. He was also required to keep in as much shadow as possible, and there wasn't too much shadow. On the other hand, it wasn't Blackpool Illuminations. Two street lamps, of meagre wattage, but it was a short street — a cul-de-sac, in fact — with a grimy stone wall at one end, a handful of long-condemned terrace houses along one side and, opposite them, the windowless wall of a warehouse.

Part of Charlie Beat, better known as Adamson's Patch, and a grimy little crumb of the latest "community policing" gimmick. Which (again, in the considered opinion of P.C. Adamson) was so much crap. This glorified rat-hole was a particularly unsavoury corner of a larger Arab quarter whose official designation was North End Division which, in turn, was part of the old Lessford City police area. But that, too, had changed. Some lunatic or another (by this time, no doubt some *Sir* lunatic or another) had obviously taken an Esso Road Map into a dim recess within the Whitehall corridors of power, licked his pencil and drawn squiggly lines as the fancy had taken him. The result? Lessford Metropolitan Police District; a monumental dog's dinner which encompassed the old Lessford City force, the old Bordfield Force and damn near all the surrounding county constabulary. Jesus wept! It had been like bringing back the Age of the Dinosaurs. The impression was that lowly coppers had disappeared into the maw of this newly-created monster and never been seen again.

And now this "community policing" lark. Having created a force ten times too big to handle, they'd grated it down into slivers and handed each sliver to some miserable flatfoot and said, 'There you are, mate. That's yours. Learn it and love it. Make believe you're a village bobby. Get to know everybody. Become their friend. Grow to be their own private pig. Aren't you lucky!'

Thus Charlie Beat and, as far as Adamson was concerned, he'd have exchanged it for a den of slavering hyenas any day of the week.

Mind you, he'd put up a fight.

'I'm not living there, sir.'

'It's necessary, constable. You can't possibly know what's going on unless . . .'

'I'm buying my own house up near Mellor Road, sir.'

'People have been known to sell a house and buy another.'

'In North End?'

'You've a duty to the force, Adamson.'

'I've a duty to a wife and daughter, sir. That lass of mine isn't going to mix with the young slags of *that* neck of the woods. With a bit o' luck she might end up at university. I'm not going to . . .'

'And if I make it an order?'

'Resignation, sir.'

Two words. That's all it had needed. It had done the trick, but since then Adamson had wondered. Supposing the gaffer *hadn't* softened? Up a gum tree, that's where he'd be. Fifty years old, "unskilled labour" and not a snowball's chance in hell of landing anything better paid that night-watchman. God, he'd chanced his arm! Since then, he'd walked on eggs without too much argument. Even when Ballester had come up with *this* particularly cockeyed scheme.

Nevertheless, Cutter. Tich Cutter, big-time crook. Somebody needed urgent skull surgery.

Tich Cutter hadn't the brains to open a jam jar, for sure he'd turn the top clockwise. A self-styled jockey, in the past he'd pulled nags and lost races on the worst tracks in the country. To say he was a has-been would be a gross exaggeration. He never *had* been. But today nobody in his right mind would allow Tich Cutter within ten miles of a horse; on principal it would have kicked his head clear of his shoulders as part-reprisal for what he'd done to its equinine pals. These days he pulled pints on Saturday nights behind the bar of The Bunch of Grapes. The rest of the week he spent most of his time mooching around street corners, exchanging race-talk with morons who knew even less about horses than he did.

From somewhere he'd found energy enough to father two sons. At the moment, both were inside on mugging charges. Like their father, they were thick. Maybe even thicker than he was. They hadn't even had the simple gumption to stick to little old ladies. The girl friend of a local karate instructor, no less, and she was no beginner at the game. Added to which, the man in her life was out of sight only because he'd stopped to buy an evening newspaper. Even the Crown Court judge had raised a frosty smile as he'd handed out a oncer on each count; he could afford to smile, he hadn't a smashed collar bone and a broken nose, and he wouldn't limp for the rest of his miserable life.

As for Ma Cutter? She was the only member of the family with muscles. But the I.Q. remained the same. Adamson had received the shock of his life when he'd delivered the news of her sons' conviction. 'Do 'em good. Make men of 'em.' Thus maternal affection, Cutter style.

And this was the family, the head of whom (according to Ballester) was up to the ears in a Crown Jewel job. Christ! At a guess, Ballester couldn't detect his way from one end of a drainpipe to the other.

Adamson jerked the collar of his overcoat a little higher, then bent to check that the copy of the *Daily Mirror* tied around each calf (under the trousers, beneath the stockings and on top of the long johns) hadn't slipped out of place. He glanced at his watch. It was almost ten minutes past ten and, as he knew from past experience, Tich Cutter was something of a night owl.

As he tucked the cuff of the glove back into position the first flurry of snow arrived, and the Adamson cup runneth over.

Chamber's Court — which was where the Cutter family lived — had a mere five houses; two-up-two-down back-to-back monstrosities which no self-respecting dog would have called home. The Cutters lived in the fourth house. The third house was occupied by Solly Daniels and, as Adamson was keeping an eye on the Cutter place, so Solly was keeping an eye on Adamson.

Solly Daniels wasn't a bad guy. Indeed, as far as Charlie Beat was concerned — as far as the whole of North End Division was concerned —he should have sported a halo and wings. A balding Jewish gentleman, he minded his own and expected other people to mind theirs. He had no enemies — come to that, he had no friends, only acquaintances — but he had a weakness, and that weakness was cards. Specifically, solo whist. Every night for years. Solly and three fellow-enthusiasts. Not always the same three, but at The Bunch of Grapes he could always rustle up enough for a school, then trot home and play until the small hours. Sometimes, until a grimy dawn lightened the rectangle of thin curtains at the window. It was a harmless enough pastime. No fortunes were ever won or lost. A hobby. A game. Maybe an addiction. But, if so, an addiction without bad after-effects.

Until last Saturday . . .

Solo whist. So, what was solo whist? A game — a card game — what else? Like poker. Like pontoon. Why the aggravation? Less than 50p in the pot and Sammy had made a bad call. So, what was a bad call? And what if it was the third bad call of the session? So what? It hadn't been a World Championship. Nothing like that. Nobody was going to retire to some tax haven with 50p. A quiet game of solo, and Sammy had made his third bad call. Big deal! That *that* was likely to trigger off World War III.

But *almost*.

Okay, Reg had a temper. Catch him one way and he could be nasty. But, damn, he *knew* Sammy. Knew how Sammy played. Sammy couldn't play "adundance declared" if he had one suit

13

and every ace and picture card in the pack. That was Sammy's game. Reg *knew* that. It was a laugh, see? It had always been a laugh. Count Sammy in, and anything could happen. But that was okay. Nobody took Sammy too seriously. Sammy playing solo was a giggle. Sammy doing *anything* was a giggle. God had short-changed him on brains. As easy as that, but no harm in the poor guy. And, goddam it, Reg knew this. So why the aggro?

Why the smack in the mouth? And, please God, why did Sammy have to skid back in the chair, fall over backwards and catch his crust on the corner of the gas oven? Why that? Why did he have to croak so easily? And why here?

A lot of questions. A lot of nasty questions. But the nastiest question of all was Adamson. What, in hell, was he doing hanging around a dump like Chamber's Court every night? He was *there*. Every night.

Saturday night he'd been there. Sunday night he'd been there. Tonight he was there. What was with the sudden interest in Chamber's Court all of a sudden?

Saturday night. Please God there'd never be a night like Saturday night to live through again. Reg ranting away, blaming Sammy for dying so easily. Blaming *Sammy,* for God's sake! As if Sammy had croaked just to do Reg a bad turn. Jimmy tooling around trying to give the kiss of life. The kiss of life to a goddam corpse. To a stiff with a caved in skull. That Jimmy should be able to perform such miracles to order!

They'd seen Adamson as they'd arrived at the house for the card session. All four of them. They'd all seen him. They'd said Hello, but he hadn't answered. Out of uniform, too. Shuffling around in the shadows, making believe he wasn't there. Cops. Who could understand cops? Cops did crazy things for no damn reason at all. That they were cops was reason enough.

And after Sammy had gone, Adamson had still been there. And *that* hadn't added to the general joy. Jimmy had suggested nipping out and telling him. Just a suggestion. Just the once, then even he'd seen the stupidity. 'Hey, dumb-bell, he's *dead*. It's not just a nose bleed. I give him a quick push and he stiffens on us. You think any cop's gonna believe *that?*

'Even *I* don't believe that. That was no push. You thumped him in the chops.'

'Look! Look!' He (Solly) had tried to drag the ship back onto an even keel. 'We don't need no Adamson. What else we need, Adamson we *don't* need. Just straighten the poor guy. Make him comfortable. Move the blood. Then, we sit down, have a quiet beer and think about it.'

That had been Saturday. Closing up midnight. And, two hours later, Adamson had still been there. Reg and Jimmy had been ready to move out, and Sammy was still there.

He was *still* there.

My God, what do you do when you have an unwanted corpse on your hands? That, and a cop camping out on your doorstep? Assuming he (Solly) could move Sammy out on his own — which he couldn't, but assuming he *could* — the daylight hours weren't even in the reckoning. Kids slinging snowballs and making slides. People coming and going all the time. Even shortly after dark, up to the time the boozers closed. No way! Waltzing around the streets with a stiff in your arms. Even in North End it might raise a few eyebrows and a few questions. So, well after dark, but well after dark brought Adamson back into the picture.

Which was why Solly Daniels was peeking from behind curtains, in a darkened room, and watching the vague outline of Police Constable Adamson. Why Solly Daniels was watching and worrying. Because he'd seen neither hide nor hair of either Reg or Jimmy since that awful Saturday night, and Sammy was starting to stink a little.

Introducing Police Constable Ellis. Ellis was to North End what the Bloody Tower was to London. He was damn near a tourist attraction. Ellis had cut his constabulary teeth on North End when Sullivan had ruled that division with an iron fist inside a steel glove; when "bobbying" that particular hell hole had been a fancy name for waging war, twenty-four hours a day with a criminal element who only asked a copper the time if they wanted to steal his watch. Rioting? The old-time North Enders had invented that pastime. Invented it, perfected it and turned it into an art form. Nor had they needed a reason. Bouncing flatfoots around. That had been reason enough. And when the flatfoots bounced back, that was great. It added spice to life. The name of the game. Thump and *be* thumped.

Happy days!

Well, Sullivan was out of it. He'd left his mark along with a whole sackful of legends, and disappeared into the sunset. The do-goodery clowns had moved in and, North Enders being what they were, the gravy train had been welcomed as an easy rip off, without the complication of suffering sore heads and broken bones. These days crime statistics could raise the roof on its hinges and nobody cared. Mugging? Who cared about mugging? Being mugged was a way of life. What was blood there for but to be spilled? And being of a financial turn of mind, the North Enders figured that sloshing somebody across the back of the head with a blunt instrument, then taking what cash was available, was the obvious way to beat inflation.

P.C. Ellis figured these as self-evident truths and was prepared to voice them with or without encouragement. Which was why he'd never made sergeant, but was also why he was one of a bare handful of uniformed coppers capable of walking into the flying fists and boots of a North End Special and coming out at the other end a mite bloody but in no way bowed.

'When?' he asked bluntly.

As he grunted the question Ellis pulled a stapled wad of scrap paper across the surface of the public counter to within easy reach. Ellis had oil in his lamp. Nothing — but *nothing* — earned official documentation at first telling. Some right cock-and-bull yarns were spun across the public counter of North End nick. Shove the original garbage into your notebook or, worse still, onto an official form, and you ended up dripping egg yolk from your chin end. The only safe way was to shove it down on scrap paper then, if it all added up to one big fat belch, you could always burn the bloody stuff and forget it.

The woman said, 'Saturday night. He nipped out for a pint.'

'Oh, aye?'

'I haven't seen him since.'

'Sammy Gatling.' Ellis scrawled the name onto the top sheet of scrap paper. 'I know him. No need to describe him. What was he wearing?'

The woman told him, and Ellis wrote it down.

'Time did you expect him back?'

'Well — y'know — the pubs throw out. Then, happen.'

'Only "happen"?'

'He sometimes stays out all night,' she admitted without hesitation.

'What doing?'

'I don't ask.'

'Tupping?' said Ellis, without expression.

'Happen.'

'You don't ask,' murmured Ellis.

'No.'

'He's well past the twenty-one mark,' mused Ellis. 'There isn't a warrant out for him. Owt like that. There's not a lot we can do, missus.'

'He's a wife and five kids.' Her eyes blazed a little.

'A "wife"?' Ellis raised an eyebrow.

'As good as. We haven't been officially churched, but . . .'

'It makes a bit of a difference. Not all that much these days, but *we're* still old-fashioned.'

'I want him back.'

'*I* haven't got him,' said Ellis innocently.

'You know what I mean.'

'Old lass.' Ellis dropped his pencil onto the surface of the counter. He'd learned all he needed to know. The usual North End crap, and who could blame Sammy Gatling for taking a one-way ride to freedom with five kids and this sloppy-looking cow waiting on the hearth-rug. Nevertheless, his voice was not too unkind as he said, 'He's blown. That's my guess. Not right. Very naughty of him. But he's well past the age of consent, and knocking five nippers out of you doesn't make him your husband. So? It's a hard world, old luv, but *we* have to live it strictly by the book. Whoever else you want, you don't want a copper.'

'What if he's been done in?' she asked, without emotion.

'Any reason to think he has?'

'No. But . . .'

'If he has, call again.'

That was Tuesday, December 15th, and that afternoon Solly Daniels left his home to seek out certain card-playing buddies. He was wise enough not to waste time calling at their respective homes. They were both "on the social", which meant they both moved as far away from their complaining wives as possible during the day. They were, however, warm-blooded animals, therefore they needed shelter. The pubs were enjoying their afternoon break and had kicked all their customers out into the

17

snow. The choice of warm spots, therefore, was limited.

He found Jimmy Holmes in the Reading Room of the local branch of the public library.

It was a cosy, single-storey building and, other than the local nick, the only "free admittance" place open to the public in North End which boasted central heating. Strangely, it was treated with a modicum of respect. The newspapers, barred securely to waist-high reading desks, were rarely torn. The magazines and periodicals, each in its own thin plastic folder, remained reasonably clean. There were reasons. The few North Enders who used the Reading Room for its designated purpose guarded it with an almost furious jealousy; to them it represented temporary escape from an immediate world they wished to forget. It was their Alice's looking-glass — more real than the glossy make-believe of the telly — and they allowed nobody to mist it or chip it and thus sully their daily dose of vicarious jet-setting and high-living. As for the others — those who rarely entered the Reading Room — they were of a society terrified of the printed word. To them, the pen really *was* mightier than the sword in that they could understand violence, but logical argument or good prose was well beyond their ken. When they sidled into the Reading Room — if that was the only way to obtain the knowledge they sought — it was merely to glance at the back page of the nearest newspaper, check what had won the three-thirty then leave, hoping their presence hadn't been noticed.

The Reading Room was previously untrod territory as far as Jimmy Holmes was concerned. Solly found him leafing his way through one of the magazines, "looking at the pictures". Solly slipped a periodical from one of the racks, pulled a chair close and, from the corner of his mouth, muttered, 'You two left me in the schnook, didn't you?'

'Why no girlie mags?' murmured Jimmy.

'We can't talk here.'

'I don't want to talk *anywhere*.'

'Look, you can't . . .'

'Nowhere!' hissed Jimmy.

The truth was, Jimmy Holmes was in a bad way. It was obvious he hadn't shaved since Solly had last seen him. By the looks of him, he hadn't even undressed. Maybe hadn't even washed. His hand, as it turned the pages of the magazine, trembled slightly.

'It ain't going to go away,' whispered Solly.

'I don't know what you're talking about.'

'You know damn well . . .'

'I don't *want* to know.'

Solly opened the pages of his periodical and breathed, 'Where's Reg?'

'I don't know.'

'You two think you're going to . . .'

'I don't *want* to know.'

Solly took a deep breath, then murmured, 'Okay. I go to the cops.'

The trembling of the hand increased, but Jimmy Holmes didn't answer.

'I have to get rid of Sammy,' Solly insisted.

'See Reg,' groaned Jimmy Holmes softly.

'You say you don't know where . . .'

'The tripe-dressing place.'

'Holy cow!' Solly blew out his cheeks. Then in a harsh, determined whisper, he said, 'You stay here. Y'hear me? When I come back, I want you to be still here. If not, I go straight to the cops.'

At about this same time, Adamson crawled reluctantly from his bed. He yawned, scratched himself, then padded across the landing to the bathroom. Already the landing was festooned with tinsel and sprigs of imitation holly. The decorations continued down the staircase and into the hall and, as Adamson knew, the front room looked more like a kid's grotto than the home of a decent, self-respecting copper. May and her bloody ideas!

All right, she had brains. She was at a good school. She soaked up knowledge like a dry sponge. Chances were she'd end up at some university, and come out with enough qualifications to land her a job at any school she fancied. She was a good kid, and he was proud of her. She'd make a damn good teacher because, already, she was dotty about youngsters. But why this? Why turn the bloody house into a fire hazard just because Christmas was coming up?

Christmas. So? Christmas? As far as *he* was concerned it boiled down to one Christmas more and one Christmas less. Charlie

Beat at Christmas had to be experienced to be believed. Men who couldn't afford an arse to their pants — men on the knock and on the cadge, from year end to year end — pissed out of their stupid minds. Where the hell did they get it from? Booze cost money, and they *hadn't* any money. Or they *shouldn't* have money. But it came from somewhere. Enough money to buy booze till it slopped out of their ear-holes. Yelling, bawling, fighting. Last Christmas . . . Oh, boy! *Last* Christmas. Christmas Eve, and he'd congratulated himself on pointing all the boozed-up lunatics towards their beds; nobody gets nicked for rowdyism, or being sloshed, or even enjoying a friendly punch-up at Christmas. The unwritten Police Law. Everybody bends over backwards to keep the cells empty at Christmas. So — okay — he'd been a good little copper. He'd jollied everybody along, splashed goodwill to all men in every direction and, eventually, watched his personal flock of black sheep disappear into their respective pens. After 2 a.m. Almost 2.30 a.m. Charlie Beat had, at last, grown quiet. So, he'd lighted a cigarette and given himself five, prior to taking up his patrol until knocking off time at 4 a.m. Then he'd heard this noise. Two noises, in fact. The faint sound of a drunken voice singing — muttering, really — a bawdy version of The First Noel and, much louder, the sound of an overflow running like the clappers. Very puzzling, and he'd strolled along to investigate.

And what had it been? Some filthy, dirty bastard with a bursting bladder. He'd opened the sash window of his bedroom and was happily pissing out into the street. And Adamson hadn't tumbled till he'd been baptised. That was Charlie Beat, mate. That was North End. Bloody animals, every last one of 'em.

Well, this year they'd get Christmas. This year? Let anybody — let *one* of 'em — say a word out of place, and his feet wouldn't touch. This year, he'd give 'em a Christmas they'd remember for the rest of their miserable lives.

Mind you . . .

This home of his. This nice little semi he was busting a gut to pay for. May was decking it out like Blackpool Pleasure Beach. A socking great Christmas tree shedding pine needles all over the best carpet. *And* fairy lights. *And,* if he hadn't put his foot down, she'd have left the damn things lit all night. 'It's Christmas, daddy. You have to make it *look* like Christmas.'

'Aye, and when I get the electricity bill *that'll* look like

Christmas, an' all.' And, damn it, Kath hadn't been on his side, either. She hadn't said anything, but the "feel" had been there. Eggs for onions they switched the bloody lights on the minute he turned the nearest corner.

Bugger Christmas!

He trundled his sourness into the bathroom, stripped off his pyjamas then caught sight of himself in the full-length mirror Kath had insisted must be part of the bathroom fittings. Not bad. Not bad at *all*. For the half-century mark better than might have been expected. No Adonis, of course, but on the credit side, no tub. That bloody great scar; puckered and healed to hell where some "hanger-door" surgeon had damn near sliced him in two performing what he'd laughingly called an appendicectomy. But — y'know — scars tended to push the virility image a notch or two higher. Hopefully. The old legs and arms a bit skinny; not *quite* the muscles they used to have, but no flab. And as for the you-know-what. Well, age took its toll on most things. But not dead yet, eh? Still in good working order when needed. Kath could bear witness to *that*.

He grinned at his reflection a little shame-facedly. Like a bloody kid, admiring himself. Like a randy young kid.

He turned his back on the mirror, ran hot water into the bath, added a liberal helping of May's fancy bath oil and, in no time at all, was soaking away what remained of his previous ill-temper.

Cows innards. The guts — the throw-away part — when they dropped some old beast at the abattoir. That area where all the cow-shit was manufactured. And, if you had any doubts, take a deep breath.

Solly Daniels swallowed his nausea and stepped into the dressing shed. Three massive vats took up much of the floor space; vats which bubbled and spat clouds of evil-smelling steam. Some of the steam escaped from the open window and door, but most of it condensed and ran down the walls to soak into the mud-coloured floor. A silent, morose man with a half-smoked, unlit cigarette dangling from his lips moved steadily from vat to vat. At each vat he paused, grasped a length of timber shapped like a long-bladed oar and heaved the stewing mess into less sluggish motion.

In a corner of the shed Reg Innes sat on an upturned beer

crate and watched the man at the vats as if hypnotised at the sight of a fellow-being engaged in soul-destroying labour.

Solly hurried over, and said, 'Reg.'

'Oh, hello.' Innes looked up, then jerked his head at the vats, and added, 'They eat that shit.'

'It's about Sammy.'

'It comes in here, like mucky rugs. They boil it. Clean it. Then people buy it and eat it.'

'Sammy. We have to . . .'

'National dish in Lancashire, so they tell me. They must be bloody mad.

'Sammy Gatling,' hissed Solly, glancing at the man stirring the contents of the vats.

'What about him?' The surprise looked quite genuine.

'For God's sake!'

'He's dead.'

'You *killed* him.'

'There was an accident. He's dead.' Innes kept his voice low, but the menace was there to hear. 'Don't start talking about "killing". People might get the wrong idea.'

'Reg.' Solly squatted down on his heels in order to bring his face level with that of Innes. He watched the man at the vats and tried to ignore the stench and the steam as he said, 'Reg, I don't care how he died. Just that he's dead. Just that he's still at my place, and I want him moved. That's not unreasonable.'

'Not unreasonable,' agreed Innes.

'So I want him out.'

'Okay. Where?'

'You tell *me*. Jimmy's waiting at the Reading Room. I warned him — I'm warning *you*, Reg — I want Sammy out of my house, or I go to the cops.'

'They'll ask questions.' For the first time Innes looked worried.

'I'll answer those questions. I go to the cops, I tell the truth. What do I lose? They chew me up a little for not telling them sooner. Other than that, what do I lose?'

'I'm in it.' Innes glanced at the vats. 'Like being in one of those things. I'm up to the ears.'

'Convince them it was an accident.'

'My aching back!'

Solly Daniels suddenly realised that Reg Innes was something

22

of a mental mutation. Having lived all his life in North End, Solly thought he'd met just about everything. Villains, tearaways, twisters, liars, the lot. You name it — you name the swindle or the outrage — and Solly would have placed his hand on his heart and sworn to his own personal God that he could put a name to a man or a woman who had pulled that swindle or committed that outrage. But as far as Solly Daniels was concerned, Reg Innes was unique. A one-off job. He was evil without even *knowing* he was evil. Sammy Gatling was dead. Considerably dead. He was even starting to pong. More than that and, whether or not it had been an accident, Reg Innes had killed him. At the very least, responsible for Sammy being dead. *And it didn't mean a damn thing.* It didn't matter that Sammy was dead, it didn't matter that Sammy had been killed, it didn't matter that Sammy's body was still above ground and gently rotting away in a room in Chamber's Court. He wasn't scared. He wasn't worried. He wasn't even unduly *interested*.

It was amorality gone mad.

Solly moistened his lips then, in a very deliberate tone, said, 'Reg, Sammy has to be shifted.'

'Sure.' Innes nodded mild agreement.

'Soon.'

'Sure,' repeated Innes.

'And I mean *soon*. Tonight.'

'There's Adamson.'

'I been watching Adamson,' said Solly, in as steady a voice as he could manage. 'He comes on about eight. Goes off about four. Most of the time, he just stands there. It has to be after four.'

'Tonight?'

'Tonight,' insisted Solly. 'Four o'clock in the morning.'

'Sure.' Innes watched the man stirring the mess in the vats. 'Where to?'

'Eh?'

'You want him moving. Where to?'

'I don't give a damn,' breathed Solly desperately. 'Just out of my house.'

'Tonight?'

'Tonight or I go to the cops.'

'Nowhere in particular?'

'Reg, nowhere. Anywhere! Just out of my house. Tonight.'

'Sure.' Innes sucked at his teeth contemplatively. 'I'll think of somewhere.' He stared at the steaming vats for a moment, then added, 'Christ! They *eat* that stuff, with chips.'

Be it understood, Johnstone was no Sullivan. Their single common denominator was that they both were, or had been, uniformed chief superintendents responsible for North End Division. Myths and legends had already been woven around the now retired Sullivan, but no myths or legends would ever have Johnstone as their centrepiece. Johnstone had reached chief superintendentship via a well-trodden route; by carefully saying Yes and No to the right people at the right moment. He never argued with a superior. Equally, he never agreed with an underling. Indeed, he neither argued nor agreed with *anybody* unless, and until, he knew exactly which side of the fence the cat was likely to land. If possible, he waited until the cat had actually landed before committing himself to an opinion. He would never be a great policeman, he would never even be a good policeman and, for much of his life, he wondered why. He was a vaguely unhappy man, and this, too, puzzled him. He had a good job, a good salary, a fine house and a fat pension awaiting him when he retired, but all these things seemed less than he desired. The sad fact was, he was not a complete fool — although he often acted and talked like one — and a grain of truth at the back of his mind nagged at his thoughts and forever insisted that what respect he was given rested upon the rank he carried — upon the crowns and baubles on his uniform — and not at all upon himself as a man.

His manner was pompous. His carriage was pompous; despite slanderous whisperings, he did not wear a corset, he merely held himself as if he *was* wearing a corset. He was without humour, and the simple fact was that, because he never laughed at himself, he was often laughed at by other people behind his back. Not friendly laughter, but laughter laced with contempt for a dwarf occupying a giant's chair.

He raised the roneoed Headquarters Circular an inch or so, then allowed it to fall back onto the surface of his desk as he looked up at the man summoned to his office.

'Fowl patrol, chief inspector. From tonight until New Year's Eve, inclusive.'

24

'Fowl patrol, sir?' King couldn't hide his surprise.

'Theft from poultry farms. There's an annual increase just before Christmas.'

'Yes, sir. But . . .'

'Orders from headquarters. Fowl patrols to be organised.'

'Sir, there aren't any poultry farms in North End.'

'I'm aware of that, of course.'

'Those circulars.' King moved his head in a single nod. 'They're sent out every year. One to every D.H.Q. I think they're only meant to be acted upon by divisions which *have* poultry farms in their area.'

'We receive a circular, King. It sets out specific instructions. We obey those instructions.'

'But sir, if . . .'

'We obey instructions, Chief Inspector King. We don't argue. We don't take a head count. Headquarters demand a fowl patrol. We give them a fowl patrol.'

'Yes, sir,' sighed King.

'As from tonight.'

'Yes, sir. I'll get it under way.'

King left, strolled along corridors and ended up in the Charge Office. He shared his problem with the duty sergeant, Sergeant Lowe.

'Which poultry farms?' asked Lowe in a puzzled voice.

'Generally. Not specifically.' King felt morally obliged to minimise Johnstone's stupidity as much as possible. 'It's possible the thieves might be from this division. We might intercept them on the way home.'

'Might,' agreed Lowe doubtfully. Then, as if to underline that doubt, added, 'Possibly.'

'A token turn-out, sergeant,' sighed King.

'How many, sir?'

'More than one.' The feather-light emphasis on the final word was not lost on the duty sergeant.

'Two?'

'That should suffice. Who have you in mind?'

'Adamson. He's on some hit-and-miss observation duty on his own beat. I'll have a word with Sergeant Ballester. He might as well be looking for nicked turkeys.'

'And?'

25

Lowe pondered a moment, then said, 'Ellis. He was off at two, but he won't mind. Give him a bit of cheap overtime. That way we won't rob Peter to pay Paul. Ten till two a long enough stint?'

'Ten till two,' agreed King. 'Ask them to use Ellis's car, then claim mileage allowance.'

Late that afternoon, snow began to fall again. Great 10p-sized flakes, drifting slowly from a sky heavy with more to come. It fell, lay and added more depth to the snow already there. The ploughs and the gritters pushed their way through the main streets and roads, but the lesser thoroughfares of the city were left to choke, pending a break in the latest blanketing. With this new fall the frost eased a little, and people relieved of the immediate need to keep warm remembered that Christmas really *was* upon the point of exploding. In the closed market otherwise sane men haggled about the price of holly; counting the berries (or lack of them) and hoping to adjust the asking-price accordingly. The hot-pie-and-peas stall did a roaring trade. Fresh turkeys hung, like feathered balloons, from every butcher's rail. The fruiterers sold their produce as fast as they could bag it. It was as if the whole city was laying in for a prolonged siege.

In the Adamson household, Kath and May had arrived home loaded with bags and parcels, snatched a quick meal, then gone out again to purchase yet more presents and goodies. Adamson had watched and not all his objections had been feigned. 'Hey, lass, is every other bloody pupil at that school of yours a "best friend"?'

'Daddy, you can't be cheese-paring at Christmas.'

'Can't I? Just you watch, girl.'

'Ignore him, darling. He's in one of his broody moods.' Which was *it*. Wife or daughter and he might have stood a chance, but wife *and* daughter was well beyond any man's capabilities. A sickly grin and unconditional surrender gave the only hope of retreat with even a modicum of dignity.

Sammy Gatling's common law wife coped as well as she was able. It wasn't that she missed Sammy. Men! Christ, most of the time their feelings never went higher than their crotch, and five kids was enough for any woman, but because they hadn't bothered to make it legal things might get a bit sticky when she

26

applied for extra "social". She was entitled to some extra. She was bloody sure she was *entitled* to some extra. It sounded sense, what with Christmas coming up and Sammy leaving everybody in the lurch like this. But to *get* that extra she'd have forms to fill in. Bet your bloody life there'd be forms. Yards of forms. And some silly young cow, still with nappy marks round her arse, ready to say they'd been filled in all wrong. Maybe the Sal Gash though, eh? *They* didn't need forms. The good old Sal Gash. Good for a quick hand-out any day of the week, especially at Christmas. No questions asked. Bit of luck and there might be one of them food parcels for good measure. So, up *you* Sammy Gatling, wherever you are. And if you've found some tart daft enough to take you on, up *her* an' all.

Poor old Sammy Gatling. To have unwittingly caused so much trouble, and not even be aware of the fact.

But he was being talked to. In death, he was being sympathised with far more than he'd ever been sympathised with in life. Solly had collected Jimmy Holmes and taken him back to Chamber's Court. Nor had Solly been open to reason. 'I should care where your wife thinks you are. I should worry. I'm not a hard man, Jimmy, but I can be pushed too far. This time it's too far. I've warned Reg — I've given him fair warning — he'll be along to collect. Tonight some time. When it's safe. But *you're* coming with me. I don't even go *near* Sammy again without somebody with me. You think I'm Dracula, maybe? Like living with dead bodies?'

And now they were back in Solly's home, and Solly was talking to Sammy Gatling, as if Sammy Gatling was still alive and capable of understanding. It made ice creep down Jimmy's spine.

'It's okay, Sammy. We'll put you somewhere nice tonight. You'll see.' He bent and straightened the soiled collar at the neck of the corpse. 'Reg, see? He can fix things. He'll fix it fine.'

'Hey, Solly.' Jimmy Holmes's voice was a trembling whisper. 'He can't hear. He's dead. He's even starting to stink.'

'You know he can't hear?' Solly's tone bordered upon the belligerent. As if he was arguing on behalf of the dead man. 'You *know*, for a fact? You been dead, maybe? You *know*?'

'Solly, he's . . .'

'I spent three days telling him how sorry I am.' Solly looked up from where he was squatting alongside the corpse. There was a hint of fanaticism in his glare. 'All this. Reg hitting him, like he shouldn't. Killing him. You think he shouldn't be told? You think he should be made to work it out for himself? Now he knows, eh? Now he knows we didn't mean to kill him. Didn't mean to leave him here. It helps a little. It helps him to understand.'

Jimmy Holmes breathed, 'Oh, my Christ!'

Adamson was back in uniform. A telephone call from D.H.Q. had brought him on duty at six o'clock; three hours normal patrol duty on Charlie Beat, then a meal, then pick up Sam Ellis and ride around in Ellis's motor car. Every night until New Year's Eve. Money for old rope. Boxing Day his day off. Nice, that. Boxing Day was the one day of the holiday when young May hadn't organised a ram-sammy at home; every other day — Christmas Eve, Christmas Day, New Year's Eve and a couple of days in-between — pop records and Coke and lunatic kids kicking up hell's delight and talking a language of their own invention. Shove *that* for a lark! Funny how Kath seemed not to mind. Seemed to even enjoy it. Not mutton-dressed-up-as-lamb enjoyment. A quiet enjoyment. A sort of "watching" enjoyment; sitting there smiling, tapping her foot in time with the pop crap, not saying much, not interfering, just letting some of the excitement rub off on her. A good lass, Kath. Growing old gracefully. Not that she *was* old. Not by a long chalk. But not bothering. Just letting it happen without souring her. God, he'd been lucky. Luckier than he deserved. He could have done a lot worse. With both Kath and May. A bloody sight worse.

Pity *he* wasn't of a like mind. Pity *he* couldn't be as tolerant. The job though, eh? Spend a small lifetime up to the armpits in conniving bastards, *that* rubs off, too. Nobody mentions *that* in the adverts. Nobody tells you *that* on your Initial Training Course. How the bloody job gets you down. How, just now and again, you're scared shitless, but haven't to show it. How the do-goodery lunatics turn everything upside down and make the hooligans heroes and don't give a damn about the poor sod bleeding his life away in the nearest gutter. All the bloody excuses in the world for things that can't be excused. You want an example? That what you want? Only last week — maybe the

28

week before — some crap-brained would-be-intellectual had argued with him about the Yorkshire Ripper. Peter William Sutcliffe, no less. That he was the product of his environment and his upbringing. Those very words. "The product of his environment and upbringing". Bullshit! He'd had a good upbringing, by comparison. By comparison to *him*, Peter Adamson, for example. Try Hunslet for size, mate. Try Hunslet, when he'd been a kid. Try Jack Lane School, where they belted you across the lug-hole for nowt. Try street after street of cobbles, row after row of back-to-back houses, and one lav shared by every four houses. Try one bath a week, in a zinc tub pulled up in front of an open fire, and the only hot water coming from a bloody great kettle balanced on a gas ring. Try *that*, mate! But it hadn't driven *him* to smashing women's skulls in with a hammer. So bugger "environment and upbringing" for a game of soldiers. Bugger *that* for an excuse. By comparison Sutcliffe had had a silver spoon in his gob. But he still had to be excused, see? He still had to be *explained*. They *all* had. Like bad mannered kids, with their parents spouting so much crap because they'd spoiled 'em rotten. And the kids loving it. Loving it, and knowing they could get away with blue bloody murder as long as the coppers were kept busy dodging accusations made by gormless nerks who didn't know what the hell they were talking about.

Like this skiving lot on Charlie Beat. Charlie Beat? Listen, mate, where *he'd* been pupped Charlie Beat would have looked like a collection of well-housed, superannuated nancy-boys.

Still — and for all that — thank God for Kath.

The thoughts and musings of a patrolling police constable who had no wish, and had never *had* any wish, to be other than what he was. A uniformed officer and one of the P.B.I. of the Police Service. A man who, despite his complaining, could handle the job and *knew* he could handle it.

A voice said, 'Merry Christmas, Constable Adamson.'

'Eh?' The greeting jolted Adamson out of his brown study.

'Merry Christmas,' repeated Reg Innes.

'Oh — er — same to you.'

Adamson eyed Innes with barely concealed suspicion. Innes was a queer customer; somebody Adamson had never quite been able to fathom. Like now. Standing there, with more than an inch of piled snow on his cap and his shoulders. No overcoat. Hands in pockets. Obviously soaked and freezing, but standing there with a half-smile on his face, ready to exchange seasonal small-talk with a uniformed copper. Innes was deep or, if not deep, *different*. Not one of the Charlie Beat run-of-the-mill yobs. Maybe this was some subtle gag. A private form of mickey-taking. If so . . .

'Haven't seen you about lately,' lied Innes.

'Been looking?'

'No. Just that — y'know — you're usually around.'

'I'm around now,' said Adamson flatly.

'Bad weather.' Innes cocked his head, and a snowflake landed in one eye and made him blink. 'Not a nice evening to be out, would you say?'

'It's what I'm paid for.'

'Aye. I reckon.'

'Dressed for.'

'Aye.'

'Not like you.' Adamson allowed a nicely timed pause to build up, then said, 'Going somewhere?'

'Home.' Innes moved a shoulder and dislodged some snow.

'Not in *that* direction.'

'Roundabout way. I've a bit of a call to make. Then home.'

'Keep out of it,' said Adamson, and it could have meant anything. It could have meant keep out of the weather. Equally, it could have meant keep out of trouble.

'Oh, aye.' Innes grinned. Then he repeated, 'Merry Christmas, Constable Adamson.'

Adamson grunted and watched the figure of Innes gradually disappear into the curtain of falling flakes. Like a ghost disintegrating. A mischievous ghost. Perhaps even a wicked ghost.

Ballester (Detective Sergeant Andrew Ballester) was of the throw-it-at-the-fan-and-let-everybody-catch-a-share school of detectives. He worked on percentages. Believe every tip-off; the law of averages insisted that *some* tip-offs delivered the Danish. Thereafter, soft pedal the goolies, make a full-scale Mahler symphony from the rest and stand by to catch the kudos. With Ballester, it worked. And why not? He was an artist at the game. He could take lifting milk bottles and, by the time the paper work had received his skilled attention, the file wasn't too many pages short of that covering the Great Train Robbery. And scrawled at the foot of every sheet was the legend *A. Ballester. D.S.* Lights and bushels? Ballester's personal, thousand-candle-power photo-flash was always at the ready, and what the hell was a bushel, anyway?

Ballester was an unloved man — even his wife hadn't been mad keen — but, given the right patter, he could be taken on an everlasting donkey ride. And no man could hoist Ballester aboard the moke with greater skill than "Jumbo" Jakeman.

"Jumbo", because the poor guy had a distinctly elephantine appearance. Not big but, proportionately, very thick limbed and with an awkward, lumbering gait. His face was flat and expressionless, his nose was squashed and broad, his ears, while not exactly flapping were, nevertheless, a little too large and protruding. In a community like North End such a man *had* to be tagged "Jumbo". The final touch was a deep, adenoidal voice; the tendency to pronounce the "n" as if it was a "d". The overall impression was mild witlessness, but that was okay by Jakeman; Jakeman's lamp was well topped-up with oil, and anybody who thought otherwise was wide open for any number of cons.

They were in a pub on the outskirts of North End. It was an old pub, still carrying the aura of its original spit-and-sawdust days, a pub dedicated to the solemn business of selling and supplying booze without the distraction of piano or jukebox. Dominoes was tolerated but, despite the rarely used board, darts was discouraged. Tippling was the only game of any standing in this place.

Ballester and Jakeman conversed softly in one corner of the taproom. It was early evening, bad weather outside and, other than the shirt-sleeved keep who lounged behind the bar-counter and minded his own business, they were alone.

'You're sure you've got it right about Tich Cutter?' muttered Ballester.

'Lay your life on it, Mr Ballester,' gurgled Jakeman.

'This weather?'

'Well — y'know — timing.' Jakeman tapped the side of his squashed nose with a forefinger. 'I don't have to tell *you*. A big job. A big lift. You can't let a bit of snow screw things up.'

'No. I suppose not.'

'When? Well, I wish I could name time, place and date.' Jakeman looked quite sorrowful. 'But — y'know — it's best not to get too nosey.'

'No! For Christ's sake don't . . .'

'Tell you what, though, Mr Ballester.' Jakeman leaned a little nearer. 'I might be able to name the day. *On* the day, if y'see what I mean. *That* day — the day it's on — let you know. Or if it's postponed. Or called off. That sort of thing. I think I might be able to get that close without making 'em sus.'

'Don't risk it, Jumbo. Don't . . .'

'Yes, I think I can, Mr Ballester.' Jakeman nodded his head slowly, as if working out the finishing touches to some careful but foolproof plan. 'I can. I *know* I can.'

'Day or night,' encouraged Ballester.

'No telephone,' said Jakeman hurriedly. 'You know me, Mr Ballester. I don't know many people with telephones. If they spot me using a kiosk every day, they'll . . .'

'Of course, of course,' agreed Ballester. 'Right. You suggest something.'

'Here?' Jakeman made it sound like a very tentative suggestion.

'Won't they . . .'

'Cutter's barred from this boozer,' lied Jakeman. 'So's most of his mates.'

'Oh!'

'I could — y'know — come a different way each day. Make sure nobody was following.'

'Still a bit dangerous, though.'

'Not as dangerous as telephoning.'

'All right.' Ballester reached a decision. The decision Jakeman had led him to reach. 'About this time, each day. That suit?'

'Best we can do, Mr Ballester.'

'I'll — er — I'll make it worth your while, Jumbo. You know me. I'm appreciative. More than most.'

'I know you, Mr Ballester.'

'That's it then.' Ballester stood up. 'Same again?'

'Aye. Thanks.'

Thus in the whole of North End no other two men were as mutually satisfied as Detective Sergeant Andrew Ballester and John "Jumbo" Jakeman. One was convinced he had that priceless conduit via which crimes galore could be detected. The other knew for a fact that, if he played his cards right, he had free booze well into the foreseeable future.

'You think he shouldn't smell?' demanded Solly. 'You think when you've been dead four days you ain't gonna smell?'

'Three days,' corrected Jimmy Holmes.

'Three days. Four days. He ain't gonna make the violets jealous.'

It was a gentle, but penetrating stench. Sweet-sour and sickly. Innes had wrinkled his nose and remarked upon it as soon as he'd entered the house.

'This man.' Solly looked down at the corpse as he continued. 'He's complaining that you smell a little. *He* is! That tripe boiling dump. Know it? That place smells. And I mean *smells*. That's where he was. And he comes in here and just because . . .'

'Hey.' Innes stared. 'You talking to the stiff?'

'All the time,' breathed Jimmy.

'What gives?' Innes looked worried.

'He wants moving.' Solly returned his attention to Innes. 'He wants moving somewhere nice. He doesn't *belong* here.'

'Okay. I'll . . .' Innes swallowed. 'Somewhere nice. Somewhere he *belongs*.'

Had the situation been merely gruesome, Innes would not have been affected. His was not a susceptible nature. To him what had once been Sammy Gatling was on a par with a lamb chop, and not a very fresh lamb chop at that. Meat on the turn, that and nothing more. But Holmes was like a jelly and Daniels was moving round the bend. Innes had problems because in the background lurked the cops, and accident, misadventure — call it what you like — for starters the cops would call it *murder*. The way their minds worked. Okay, it *wasn't* murder; it was all sorts of things, but not murder. It was Sammy Gatling's own fault for not making the right call; for not being able to read his hand right; for even playing the damn game unless he knew how. It was Solly's fault for including Gatling in the school in the first place; for not knowing that card-playing is a serious occupation, and not something to be screwed to hell by idiots who shouldn't be allowed within touching distance of a deck. All these things, but the cops would start the ball rolling by calling it murder, and what's-his-name — Ballester — Ballester was the sort of

fornicating bastard who'd stick. Innes knew Ballester. Ballester
was a bladder filled with wind and piss, but he made noises.
Loud noises. *He'd* stick with murder till hell froze. Murder,
because murder was headlines and Ballester loved headlines.
Maybe there was somebody high up who could screw Ballester
down. Maybe. Innes didn't know; he'd made a point of never
being on buddy-buddy terms with top-rank coppers. But Ballester
he knew. Ballester would fix things. Too right! Ballester hunted
glory, and Ballester had been known to work sweet little flankers
to *get* glory. So it would be murder, and it would *stay* murder
with Ballester at the wheel.

In a slightly hoarse voice, Innes said, 'Adamson's on the
pavement again.' The two looks of non-understanding made him
add, 'He's back in uniform. He's not watching . . . what the hell
he *was* watching.'

'I don't see . . .' began Holmes.

'We don't have to wait for four. Let the streets clear —
midnight, about — we can shift him.'

'Where we gonna carry him?' asked Solly sorrowfully. 'I mean
. . .'

'I got a van fixed. A bread van.'

'A *bread* van?' Holmes's jaw dropped.

'I don't have pull with people who run hearses,' said Innes
sarcastically. 'So a bread van. We take out the trays. Shelves.
What the hell they are. Shove the stiff inside.'

'Th-then what?' asked Holmes.

'Put him where he should be. That's what.'

Average cops don't exist. To maintain such a premise is a little
like taking all the colours from deep pink to blazing scarlet and
reaching an "average red". The same with cops. The bully-boys
and the softly-softly types, the mouthy and the taciturn, the ones
who look small for their size and the ones that look big for their
size, the book men and the seat-of-their-pants men, those who
wear the uniform as a shield and excuse and those who, uniform
or not, lower their heads and charge. The good and the bad, of
course, come in every shape and shade; rogue cops do not necessarily have brawn any more than they necessarily have brains and,
with equal certainty, the same can be said of men of honour.
They're all cops, and in any given force the only true uniformity

is the uniform they wear.

Some men, however, are similar. It is a similarity of character, a similarity of personality, a similarity of practicality. This similarity of certain types of officer forms the bedrock upon which a force can be built. Officers like Adamson and Ellis. Peter Adamson and Samuel Ellis thought and worked along similar lines. They were both uniformed patroling constables and content to be such; neither seeking nor requiring advancement or the pseudo-glamour of C.I.D. the better to do their job. They could feel collars with the best when the need arose, but equally they could turn a blind eye when the spirit of the law made the letter of the law read like so much crap. They had learned the knack of cutting corners, but at the same time were prepared to absorb criticism without rancour when their corner-cutting reached the notice of senior and less practical officers.

In short, they were complete and contented men, and as they sat within the comfort of Ellis's V.W. they watched the continued fall of the snow and were happy enough to waste time and be paid for it.

'Ready for Christmas?' asked Ellis.

'As I'll ever be.' Adamson chuckled quietly. 'That lass of mine. *And* the missus.'

'Funny how women like Christmas,' mused Ellis. 'Mind you, I was reading. A few weeks back. No such thing as female angels. That's what this professor bloke said. A theologian. All the pictures. All the writings. Not so much as a hint.'

'Hadn't thought about it,' admitted Adamson. 'Still, now you mention . . .'

'Funny sort of Heaven.' Ellis warmed to his subject. 'No women. All them trumpets and harps. All them choirs. Very noisy. But no women.'

'Maybe they issue ear-plugs.'

'Must be very disappointing for all them holier-than-thou biddies.'

'Eh?'

'All that charitable stuff. Then when they reach The Pearly Gates, a "Men Only" sign staring 'em in the face.'

'Oh, aye.' Adamson chuckled again.

'Might as well have enjoyed themselves. Been regular slags.'

'Happen.'

'Like Gatling's woman.' Ellis fumbled for a packet of cigarettes. 'She was in earlier today.'

'Who?'

'Gatling's piece. Common law wife, what the hell she calls herself. Smoke?'

'Ta.'

They lighted cigarettes, then Ellis continued, 'Sammy's blown. Another woman by the sound of things.'

'Oh, aye? I didn't know.'

'Saturday night. Hasn't been home since.'

'Saturday night?'

'Uhu.'

'Saw him Saturday night,' said Adamson without real interest.

'Where?'

'Chamber's Court. He was with Solly Daniels and that bastard Innes.'

'Innes?'

'A right one, that. Very smart.'

'Very sharp,' agreed Ellis sardonically. 'One day, he'll be too sharp and cut his own bloody throat.'

Thereafter, the talk veered off in a variety of directions. Words with which to pass the time pending the arrival of 2 a.m. On paper they were looking for fowl thieves, but in fact they were parked in a quiet cul-de-sac on the outskirts of North End enduring the boredom of everyday policing, while at the same time thankful to be sheltered from the weather. Come the end of the month, Ellis would do mental calculations then apply for reimbursement for the cost of petrol which *should* have been used had the V.W. trundled around the division, wearing out its tyres and risking a shunt-up in the appalling driving conditions. If he played his cards right — if he didn't push the boat too far from the shore-line — he'd be paid and no questions asked. A minor fiddle. They both knew it. They both accepted it. And why not? Chief Superintendent Johnstone had triggered the fiddle because of his own inadequacy as a divisional officer. Chief Inspector King was no mug — settled in an armchair in front of his own fire — he knew damn well what would be happening, but it was no skin off *his* nose if Johnstone insisted upon playing the sucker to practical bobbies. Fowl thieves, for God's sake! Why not go the whole hog and get a patrol under way looking for stray

Martians? Meanwhile, and strictly according to rules, Constables Adamson and Ellis "idled and gossiped" (the official terminology) and were liable to be fizzed for breaking Force Standing Orders. Supposing anybody cared. Or, to be strictly accurate, supposing anybody cared who *knew*.

It was after midnight. A new day. Wednesday, December 16th, and a mere eight full shopping days to the big blow-out. A fact of no importance whatever to poor old Solly Daniels.

Innes drove the van and Holmes and Solly squashed and shared the bucket-seat alongside the driving position. Holmes was sweating, and seemed to be having some small difficulty in breathing. Solly kept whispering, 'We shouldn't be doing this. It ain't nice to Sammy.' And who could blame him? Who could blame either of them?

Little more than fifteen minutes before Solly had insisted upon wrapping the dead Sammy in a bed-sheet. Soiled, perhaps, but a final act of decency to a man he in no way hated.

'They wrap beef up, don't they? They kill the cow, they slice it up and clean it. Then they wrap the sides up in muslin. You think we shouldn't do at least that much for Sammy?'

Innes had cracked, 'Nobody's likely to buy a rump steak from this one,' but the look in Solly's eye had been warning enough, and he'd hastily added, 'Okay. Wrap him up. But move.'

Thereafter the lifting and carrying to the van. The shelves and trays had been removed, but the floor of the van had a liberal sprinkling of crumbs from bread and cakes. With the sheet-wrapped body only part-way through the open rear doors of the van, Holmes had retched and been on the point of bringing up his heart.

Innes had grabbed at the slipping corpse and snarled, 'Get to the end of the street. Keep watch. But don't run. You run and, so help me, I'll catch you up in the van and spread you against the nearest wall.'

And, okay, you get a situation like this, you need a man like Innes. Not a nice man, not a good man, but a very *necessary* man. Somebody prepared to push and heave at something he'd once played cards with. Somebody without feelings. Somebody who didn't *care*.

Solly cared. Solly cared a whole lot. Poor Sammy Gatling —

what had once been Sammy Gatling — bumping and rolling around in the back there. Rolling around in the crumbs. Bumping against the sides of the van. Dear God, it wasn't right. It shouldn't happen to an enemy, much less a friend.

Solly croaked, 'Where are we taking him?'

'I know.' Innes peered ahead through the fan-shaped clearance where the wipers were fighting a battle with the falling snow. 'We're taking him where he belongs.'

'Home?'

'Yeah. In a manner of speaking.'

'What's that . . .'

'Shut up. It's not easy driving in this stuff.'

Not at all like the plastic cops of the silver screen, or the cathode-ray car-wreckers racing through their weekly quota of murder detection. Not at all like that. Just cold and a little bored. Cold, because the heating system of the V.W. only worked when the engine was running. Bored, because in more than two hours even a river of small-talk tended to dry into a mere trickle.

'Met Flensing yet?' asked Adamson, a propos of nothing in particular.

Ellis grunted a negative answer.

'He has 'em worried.'

'He hasn't *me* worried.' Ellis yawned and stretched his arms as far as the confines of the V.W. would allow. 'I'm not on first name terms with detective chief superintendents.'

'Different from Blayde.' Adamson seemed determined to pursue the line of conversation.

'I wouldn't know.'

'That's what I'm told.'

'Pete.' Ellis spoke as a man with a lifetime of expertise and experience to call upon. 'The rank says all, see? Always. To *get* there you have to be a one-off sod. And having got there there's only one way to stay there. Nick your own grandmother, if necessary. Use little tin soldiers like us as counters in a glorified game of Snakes and Ladders. Blayde, Lennox, this new bloke Flensing. Every last one of 'em. The only man I ever knew who didn't kid himself. Lewis.'

'Never met him. Heard of him, though.'

'A ring-tailed, double-dyed, twenty-carat bastard.'

38

'Like the others?' grinned Adamson.

'No. He never made out he *wasn't.*'

The nightmare reached its climax at the entrance to a narrow, snow-blocked lane leading to a low, dry-stone wall. On the very fringe of the division and not far from the city boundary.

Innes parked the van and said, 'We carry him from here.'

'The *cemetery*?' Holmes's question was little more than a moan.

'Where else? It's where stiffs belong. There's an open grave. They won't notice one more.'

As Innes opened the door of the van, Solly said, 'Not me.'

'All three of us.' There was a hard, uncompromising tone to Innes's voice. 'You wanted an answer, Daniels. This is the answer. Just remember *where* he died. And don't tell me you'll go to the cops. It's too late. You're in it. You're *both* in it. This way he disappears and no questions asked. And remember this — both of you — where *I* go *you* go.'

Thereafter there came the lifting and the carrying; the staggering through knee-deep drifts and the attempt to place their feet in indentations where other people had walked; the pulling and shoving over the wall; the finding of the paths which had been cleared prior to the latest covering; the lowering of the bundle into the waiting arms of Innes; the kicking down of frozen earth and the stamping and spreading of Innes as he created a false bottom to the grave and covered the wrapped body of Sammy Gatling.

Innes climbed from the open grave, kicked clinging soil from his boots, and said, 'That's it, then. If it keeps snowing, nobody's any the wiser.'

And they believed him, because things had gone well past the stage of either disbelief or argument. Only horror remained. Horror, and the trembling realisation of what they'd done.

TWO

One day some scholarly type will write a treatise concerning the various reasons why the lower income bracket citizenry almost invariably go in for the more expensive funerals. Why poverty-stricken men and women happily deny themselves small luxuries and even necessities in life in order to ensure that they have a flash send-off. The coffin; better made and far more pricey than any of the scraps of furniture they've left behind. The shroud of silk and lace, when in life they've made do with cast-offs and shoddy. The funeral tea; the obligatory nosh-up, complete with hired hall and linen table-cloths; a "sit down" job — a "knife-and-fork" do — with ham and tongue thick and juicy, with cream cakes and trifle, even with waitresses, for God's sake. As if, of itself, their poverty had been a prolonged sin to be masked behind one last attempt to con The Almighty.

And with the con, the hypocrisy.

Let him or her have been the scoundrel to end all scoundrels. Let the corpse have been a fitting companion for Old Nick himself. But despite this, eavesdrop upon the conversation at the funeral. "As nice a bloke as ever trod the face of the earth." "A lovely lass. I never knew her to say a wrong word about anybody." "By God, she'll miss him. As good a husband as you'll find anywhere." "She spoilt him, y'know. When he gets over the shock, he won't know which way to turn."

Like a hidebound, formula comedy; a black comedy bespattered with catch-phrases and running along firmly pre-determined lines.

Fred Kelly's was such a funeral. A soak in life, he was getting the full treatment now he was a customer of The Great Boozer In The Sky. At least forty sombrely-dressed mourners followed the coffin from the hearse and the row of cars parked at the gate. The top-hatted undertaker led the procession through the still-falling snow; solemn-faced and slow-paced, with secret thoughts concerning themselves with the possibility of a ten-day package holiday for himself and his wife along the Italian coast, where snow never fell and where vibrant life contrasted with his own

43

deadly profession.

'I'm — I'm sorry, sir.'

A donkey-jacketed grave-digger, still carrying a snow-encrusted shovel stepped in front of the cortege. There was a wildness in his eyes, and the impression was that his mouth was opening and closing too much for the words he was speaking.

The undertaker looked up, frowned, but continued his forward progress.

'You — you can't, sir.'

'What?'

'There's — there's a — there's another one in, sir.'

'What?'

The undertaker stopped and raised a hand, as if to halt traffic. The four assistants carrying the coffin continued to shuffle forward and the end of the coffin nudged the undertaker's top hat, tipping it forward slightly, before the procession shunted to an untidy standstill.

'What the devil?' hissed the undertaker.

'Me and Alf, my mate,' gabbled the gravedigger. 'Early, see? To shift the snow from the bottom of the grave. And — and there's *another*.'

'Another what?'

'Another body. In the grave. Another body.'

'Another coffin?' The question fairly sizzled with outrage; that some fool had lowered a coffin down the wrong hole; that some utterly incompetent fellow-undertaker had . . .

'No, sir. A *body*. Not a coffin. A body, wrapped up in a sheet.'

'What is it?' The cleric joined them and asked the question in a gentle, sing-song tone. 'Is something amiss, perhaps?'

'You wouldn't bloody <u>coco</u>,' breathed the grave-digger.

'A slight snag,' smoothed the undertaker, straightening his hat. 'At the grave. The weather, I think. If you'll — er — give my apologies to Mrs Kelly and the other mourners. I'll go ahead and get things put right. It won't take a moment.'

But it did. It took far longer than any "moment". Fred Kelly wasn't buried that day.

By late afternoon the company was assembled. In show-biz parlance, "a cast of thousands". First at the scene had been a panda van, then in quick succession, Detective Sergeant Ballester

44

and two detective constables; then enough hurriedly rounded-up uniformed men to seal off the cemetery; then Ballester's immediate boss Detective Chief Inspector Hoyle; more coppers, more C.I.D. types; the "corps de ballet" — the photographers, the plan-drawers and, for some unexplained reason, the finger-print-lifters — and the Serious Crime Squad; finally, the big bwana himself, Detective Chief Superintendent Flensing, Head of Lessford Region C.I.D.

As Flensing bent himself out of his car, Hoyle hurried across and said, 'We've identified the body, sir. Samuel Gatling. There was a letter in his pocket. We've not yet . . .'

'Gently, chief inspector.' Flensing closed the door of his car and shoved his hands into the pockets of his loose-fitting mac. 'Leave me *some* questions to ask.'

'Yes, sir.'

The quietly-spoken interruption was not a reprimand. Or, at least, it didn't *sound* like a reprimand. But come to that nothing Flensing *ever* said sounded like a reprimand or a criticism. He was the eternal "steadying influence". He was new to the force and as yet untried, but members of his previous force could have told tales galore about how "The Flenser" had lived up to his nickname. A tall man, thin but not gaunt, his expression conveyed perpetual boredom. Crime — murder, rape, muggings, the lot — was a drag; something to be detected as swiftly and as efficiently as possible, in order to return to the more interesting aspects of life. But in the main, and under his guidance, they *were* detected. Those droll, stone-faced utterances had left more than one smart Alec law-bender wondering how the hell he'd ended up surrounded by a prison wall.

Flensing strolled to the cemetery gates, stood with his feet planted firmly apart and gazed down the main tarmac path.

'Pathologist?' he murmered.

'On his way.' Hoyle glanced at his wrist-watch. 'Should be here any minute.'

'Very important personages, pathologists,' drawled Flensing. 'No pathologist, no corpse. No corpse, no murder.'

'Sir?' Hoyle frowned non-understanding.

'*You* say he's dead.'

'Yes, sir. Very dead. *Long* dead at a guess.'

'Murdered.'

'Everything points to that.'

'You're wrong, chief inspector.' The soft, dead-pan voice matched the stone-faced, slightly-out-of-focus stare. 'Friend Gatling is still alive and taking nourishment. It needs some clown with a stethoscope around his neck to say otherwise. It needs the palaver of an Inquest to verify he didn't die of natural causes in the comfort of his own bed.' Flensing paused, then said, 'Alice In Wonderland. It should be required reading for any budding copper.' Then, without change of tone and as if continuing the same train of thought, 'This cemetery. It's been taken out of circulation?'

'Yes, sir. Closed and sealed off.'

'The way to the grave?'

'Down the main path. It's been used too much for any chance of footprints. Then, we've taped out a route across untrodden snow. Cartons covering all unidentified footprints. The men are busy taking casts. Shellac spray so we don't disturb the snow, then plaster of Paris.'

'Elimination?'

'The two grave-diggers. We have their wellies for comparison.'

The conversation — the short, softly-spoken questions and the answers, as full as Hoyle could make them — continued for almost fifteen minutes. Flensing kept what seemed to be a jaded gaze fixed along the path leading from the gates to the rows of snow-caked graves. His expression never altered. His voice neither rose nor fell. He offered neither recrimination nor congratulation. Yet within that short period of time he learned everything that had been done and everything that was planned.

The pathologist arrived and Hoyle escorted him along the main path to the grave. A short, fussy-looking man in black and wearing a top hat moved closer. He'd been hovering in the background during the latter part of the conversation between the two detectives, and now he cleared his throat to attract attention.

'James,' he said, by way of introduction.

Flensing turned and tilted his head slowly until he was staring into the aggitated face of the undertaker.

'My name is James. Wallace James. I — er — I understand you're the senior officer present?'

Flensing neither agreed with nor denied that statement. He merely waited.

'Frederick Kelly. He should have been interred today.'

'Today?' echoed Flensing emotionlessly.

'I — er — I represent the family. Mrs Kelly. All the mourners. I'm the funeral director. Mrs Kelly — all the family — they're very upset.'

Flensing nodded ponderously.

'We — desire . . . We *demand* . . .'

James closed his mouth as Flensing slowly shook his head.

'Don't get *too* brave,' advised Flensing gently.

'What?'

'You "desire". Not you, personally. *Your* desires, *your* natural urges, *your* whims and fancies can be disregarded. The desires of the unfortunate family can be appreciated. But even they can't demand.'

'Really! I think . . .'

'No. Unfortunately you don't,' interrupted Flensing. 'A little thought might have helped. Might even have stopped you from making a fool of yourself. You're the funeral director. That means you're responsible for the funeral and that includes the grave. You're responsible for it being dug. You're responsible for it being ready to receive the coffin. It was *not* ready to receive the coffin. You failed in your responsibility. Have you explained *that* to the unfortunate widow?'

'That's — that's ludicrous!'

'A personal opinion. But there again on your own admission, you don't think.'

'I can't stand guard over an open grave all night.'

'You took a risk. You people always take that risk. This time it hasn't come off. Somebody's dumped a spare body in *your* grave. You can't expect to win every time.'

The solemn-faced, softly-spoken logic flattened James more completely than any amount of bluster. The fact was, he didn't *know*. He wasn't *sure*. The way this tall, self-assured policeman argued it, it seemed obvious. But he didn't *know*. Good God, you always dug the grave the day before. You *expected* it to be ready. Snags? Of course you encountered snags. You were paid to deal with snags; to smooth out the kinks; to stand by to catch some emotional next-of-kin who couldn't stand the strain; to firmly, but politely, ensure that the right people rode in the right cars; to usher around the lip of the grave only those who *should* be round the lip of the grave. All these things. What you were paid for. Not just the coffin, not just the hearse and the cars, not just the bearers. A thousand and one things that might go wrong, but that had to be put right. But, good God, the grave! You took it for granted that the grave, having been dug, would be empty. The last thing you expected was . . .

'When you apologise to Mrs Kelly,' murmered Flensing. 'When you admit that you've been highly irresponsible, give her our condolences. Assure her that *we* won't inconvenience her more than is strictly necessary.'

Solly hadn't slept. Nor (he was sure) would he ever sleep again. He wouldn't dare sleep. His waking hours were an everlasting nightmare. He was terrified to even contemplate what might creep up on him if he closed his eyes.

He sat in the bar parlour of The Bunch of Grapes. In a corner away from the fire where he knew he wouldn't be joined by other customers. He sipped his beer, but didn't taste it. He stared at the far wall, but saw only a sheet-wrapped bundle flopping awkwardly into the goo of a recently-dug grave.

By mid-evening, certain basics had been established. The obvious had been verified, reduced to writing in cold-blooded officialese and signed. The base of the pyramid, whose peak would hopefully touch the name of the killer, had been levelled and made firm. The real building could begin; the blocks hunted and, when found, fitted carefully into position.

'My way, ladies and gentlemen,' said Flensing. 'Which means dust-proof, water-proof and air-tight.'

The first briefing of the enquiry had started at a few minutes past eight o'clock. The Parade Room of North End D.H.Q. was the locale, and that same room was to be The Murder Room. 'Murder Room, ladies and gentlemen. Not "Incident Centre". I'm a little set in my ways. Indulge me. Allow me my idiosyncrasies. A dog fouling the footpath can, without exaggeration, be described as an "incident". At the moment, if we step carefully, we are not concerning with dogs fouling the footpath. Murder, if you please. Therefore, the Murder Room.' And from the moment the slim, drawling-voiced stranger had strolled centre-stage nobody had had any doubts. They listened and they heeded. They listened, because he was patently not going to raise his voice above its normal level. They heeded, because his personality demanded that there be no misunderstanding. He was the boss. Johnstone was there, of course — it was Johnstone's division, therefore courtesy demanded Johnstone's presence at the first briefing — and Johnstone was resplendent in uniform with crowns and pips, with cap complete with braided peak, but although Johnstone matched the thin man, rank-for-rank, Johnstone was a nothing. A mere ornament. An unimportant facade. He, Flensing, was top cat and the only cat of any stature in the litter.

Hoyle found himself warming to this unhurried detective chief superintendent who so obviously knew what he wanted, and was determined to get it. No bluster, no bawling here. No battering-ram tactics. Instead, a gentle but irresistible pressure which could and would eliminate all opposition with near-apologetic indifference.

'The Murder Log has already been opened. It will be kept up to date — up to the minute — under the supervision of Chief Inspector King. Any orders or instructions issued by him can be taken to be orders or instructions issued by me. Similarly, if those orders or instructions are ignored or disregarded, I shall take it as a personal disobedience and act accordingly.'

The man could delegate authority. He wasn't a one-man-band. And that, too, was unusual enough to be almost unique. Off-hand, Hoyle could name no other officer of comparabale rank who so easily, and so absolutely, handed one aspect of a major enquiry to a subordinate and, before the enquiry got under way, publicly backed that subordinate up to the hilt.

'What is known as "the field work". The day-to-day, hour-by-hour interviewing of witnesses and gathering of evidence. Detective Chief Inspector Hoyle. As with Chelf Inspector King, a decision by Mr Hoyle will be taken to be a decision by me and acted on accordingly.' Flensing paused, then added, 'Explanations, ladies and gentlemen. Not threats. The oiling of the machine. Necessary before it's put into gear. From past experience I've known some very clapped-out models limp along, and sometimes even slip into reverse, because nobody saw fit to tune it up, check

49

it and make sure it was in working order prior to it moving forward.'

Innes wanted money. This, of course, was no novel requirement; Innes had lived in a state of financial embarrassment for years. For as long as he could remember, in fact. It had never before interferred with his sleep. By his rules the time for insomnia was when people owed *you* money. The trick was to make sure *they* needed tranquillizers. But now he didn't need the odd quid, the odd fiver, the odd tenner. He needed money in bundles, and the thicker the bundles the better.

All this fuzz activity had to be side-stepped. The word "murder" was being bandied around alarmingly, and neither Daniels nor Holmes were mighty oaks strong enough to withstand the stiff breeze of a police enquiry. They'd snap at the first puff and, having snapped, they would name names. Reg Innes, for example. And more than that. Get some great, hairy-arsed copper — Ballester, for instance — leaning like the very clappers, and anything could happen. Anything! To crawl out from under. A natural reaction. What else? He, Reginald Innes, knew the score. No flies had even landed on *him*. And two-to-one were not good odds when the prize was a nerk like Sammy Gatling, who croaked if somebody gave him a gentle push.

Money, therefore. Folding stuff in large wads. Then the tall timber pending the cooling off of all this high-voltage police pressure.

'One hundred and four officers,' drawled Flensing. 'One hundred and four officers — including myself, including Chief Superintendent Johnstone — have been earmarked for this enquiry. Only those officers are allowed into the Murder Room. To everybody else it's strictly Off Limits. And I mean *everybody*. Regardless of rank or popularity. Not an unimportant point to stress. Especially at this time of year. It's warm and dry in here. It's cold and wet outside. This is a Murder Room. It is not a ready-made shelter from nature's vicissitudes.

'There are — what? — about thirty of you here. Pass the word around. We do *not* serve hot soup and sandwiches.'

Jimmy Holmes had never been more frightened in his life.

Frightened! Christ, it was having an effect upon his bodily functions. That and the weather. His bladder was filling faster than he could empty it. Every public toilet. *More.* Twice, already, he'd had to turn at the top of the steps and return to the stalls. The expression "pissing yourself". It *meant* something.

And he was trembling. Shivering. Sure, it was cold. It was December and, although the snow had eased and almost stopped, it was still brass-monkey weather. But it wasn't just the cold. Shivering from cold was one thing. Shivering from this — trembling from *this* — had damn-all to do with the temperature. It was his muscles. His stomach muscles. Even the muscles of his jaw, and his arms, and his legs. The tiny muscles quivering and twitching, making the larger muscles tremble and jerk.

Sweet Jesus, he wasn't a bad man. Not a *bad* man. Okay, no saint. He'd never claimed to be a saint. Filching a little, a couple of shopbreakings, a six-month spell inside. But not *bad.* Eva, his wife, could bear witness to that. The kids, little Jimmy, Stanley, Caroline, Shirl, baby Betsy. He hadn't been a bad father either. And they were legitimate. He'd done the right thing by Eva when Jimmy was on the way. He'd accepted *some* responsibility. She'd said he was the father and, okay, he *could* have been. A mug, maybe, but he *could* have been. So she couldn't fault him there. Maybe some randy bastard was still laughing at him. Maybe . . .

Just that he wasn't a *bad* man. Not *all* bad.

Weak. Okay, weak. The easy way out, see? Every time, the easy way out. No trouble. No aggro. Walk away from trouble, Jimmy. Walk away from it, every time. Life's not easy, so don't make it even harder by getting banjoed every so often. Let the tearaways run riot. Who cares? Just walk away. Just . . .

Then this thing had upped and smacked him in the teeth. A quiet game of cards. And now *this*.

His legs felt like jelly as he turned into one more public toilet.

Flensing continued, 'Samuel Gatling. Left home on the evening of Saturday the 12th. A quiet drink. The usual reason. Reported missing by his common law wife, on Tuesday the 15th.' For a moment the sleepy eyes rested upon the uncomfortable Ellis. 'For reasons not acceptable, but understandable, and fortunately unimportant, the report was not logged. Not important because on Saturday — later that same Saturday — he was seen in the

51

company of Daniels, Innes and Holmes. Going into the home of Daniels.

'Next sighting: dead in the opened grave of a certain Frederick Kelly. This afternoon. That is the gap we have to fill. Where he was — dead or alive — between late Saturday night and this afternoon.

'An autopsy has been performed.' The timing of the pause, followed by, 'We can, therefore, assume with some degree of certainty, that Gatling is dead,' would not have disgraced a top-line professional droll. He continued in a slow, dry-as-dust tone, 'Other words of pathological wisdom I pass on for what they are worth. Time of death. "Some few days ago". I am told that extremes of temperature play havoc with normal means of calculation. Cause of death. "Fractured base of the skull, resultant upon being struck with a blunt instrument". We must be charitable, ladies and gentlemen. Our pathologist did his best. He is no Professor Simpson. There is evidence that he was struck in the face prior to or immediately after death. Gatling . . . not the pathologist.'

Lumb — "Honest Joe Lumb" — gave Innes what he sought.

Lumb was a bookie. His father and his grandfather before him had been bookies. The solidly-built wooden hut at one corner of the rag-tag of weeds and brambles originally meant to be allotments had been the property of the Lumb family for more than half a century. Before that the main room of a terrace house (the home of "Honest Fred Lumb") had been the operational centre of this minor enterprise in catering for the wagering whims of the North Enders.

The Lumbs had specialised in off course betting. Strickly cash, and the hell with what the law had once said; an annual licence fee, in the form of a fine at Lessford Magistrates' Court, was a sight better and much more realistic than expecting North Enders to meet their gambling debts. And now, of course, it *wasn't* illegal. It was almost respectable. Joe Lumb was seriously thinking about standing at the next Council Elections and his wife was already a member of the Town Women's Guild.

All this Innes knew. He also knew that Joe Lumb was a child of North End which, in turn, meant he was only as "honest" as he *had* to be. Fiddling the punters might have been dangerous. Fiddling the tax man was like taking toffee from a three-year-old. But (the progression of Innes's logic) you couldn't fiddle the tax man *and* keep all the takings in a bank account. Do *that* and in next to no time the waters of the creek started to give off a distinctly nasty smell. Therefore, loose cash. Lots and lots of loose cash.

Innes ducked and weaved among the shadows in the rear garden of the Lumb's semi; a semi situated almost a quarter of a mile from the boundary of North End Division and in Hallsworth Hill Division. Over the years the Lumbs had come up in the world. One of the better class semi-detached properties with a fair-sized garden back, front and side. A whole lot easier to crack than a back-to-back terrace and, by the absence of lights, there for the taking.

'On the face of things,' drawled Flensing, 'we have three possible suspects. Solomon Daniels, Reginald Innes and James Holmes. The last known people to see Gatling alive. Of itself, that doesn't add up to much. But to the best of our knowledge, none of them have been home since we found Gatling's body. They *have* been home since Saturday night. Fleeting visits as far as Innes and Holmes are concerned. Mrs Innes describes her husband as being "very touchy and bad-tempered". Mrs Holmes says her husband was "sickening for something". Daniels isn't married.

'Straws in the wind, ladies and gentlemen. No more than that. So, please don't jump to conclusions. Forget Daniels, Innes and Holmes other than as "possibles". Keep things open and free-wheeling. The Golden Rule as far as this enquiry is concerned. We detect the crime, then we arrest and interview the murderer. We do *not* pick a name from the nearest hat, arrest the owner of that name, then bend the evidence to justify the arrest. None of you are innocent enough to think that hasn't been done in the past. It has. Often. But, not this time.'

Solly daren't go home. Come to that, he hadn't dared to stay at The Bunch of Grapes. Customers had come into the bar parlour. Men he knew. Friends. Men he'd played cards with in the past. Some had spotted him in the corner. One had spoken to him.

'Something wrong, Solly?'

That it should be so obvious. Something wrong. Dear God, that something *wasn't* wrong. That poor old Sammy *hadn't* accepted the invitation to the card school. That Innes hadn't even been *asked*. Something *wrong!*

He couldn't even remember leaving the pub. Just that to stay there had been so dangerous. Too dangerous. The pub talk. Talk about Sammy's body being found in the grave. Men with beer inside them. Expressing opinions. Asking questions. Asking *him* questions. And, man, he knew the answers. All the answers. *All* the answers.

And now, he daren't go home.

To go back there. To where Sammy had been all that time. To see the place where he'd sprawled. To where he'd made him comfortable, then talked to him as if he was still alive. Talked to him. Kidded himself he wasn't really dead, maybe. Kidded himself it hadn't really happened. But it *had*. And everything else had. And where in hell was it going to end?

He *daren't* go home.

He stood at the corner, pressed against the wall, and stared across the street at the uniformed, overcoated figure. The copper seeking some sort of warmth under the canopy of the Albion Bingo Hall. Fancy lights and swing-doors leading to the plush-painted foyer. Some copper seeking make-believe warmth. some copper he didn't know. A bearded copper, stamping his boots gently on the cleared pavement. One of "them".

Irrational fury rose like a tidal bore.

Coppers with beards! That it should be allowed. Some young schnook figuring himself man enough to carry a beard around. Old enough. wise enough. Like some Old Testament prophet, maybe. Like some wise old man who might be able to advise. The world was crazy. Coppers with *beards*. Somebody else —somebody like Adamson — and could be . . .

Just to be able to talk, see? Just to be able to walk across and tell somebody. Just to be able to ease the weight a little. To be able to *hope*. The man might understand. Okay, the uniform, but he *might* understand. But no creep wearing a beard — no creep not yet old enough but stupid enough to wear a beard — no way would a creep like *that* understand.

By the very nature of things, nobody ever knew. Nobody ever *would* know. But — a quirk of fate — had it been Adamson standing outside the Bingo Hall, had it even been a clean-shaven constable, and a murder enquiry would have ended on the day it begun. But — a quirk of fate — some copper had decided to grow whiskers.

'The weapon. A blunt instrument. Anything from an Aston Martin to a size ten football boot. Unfortunately, not some rare South American poison . . . in which case we'd know where to look. As it is, we have a long search. Probably a fruitless search. Nevertheless, if it's possible to find it, I want it found.

'Where was the murder committed? I'll tell you where it *wasn't* commited. At the grave. Other than that anywhere in the United Kingdom. But first we'll try to eliminate North End. Trace Gatling's movements. The narrower the gap between when he was last seen alive and when he was first seen dead, the closer we are to the grave where the body was found. Obvious? But of course. That's why I'm here, ladies and gentlemen. To remind you of the obvious. To scotch any visions of deerstalker hats and oversized magnifying glasses.

'Why was he murdered? The motive? Money was found on the body therefore, provisionally, we can discount mugging. What little we know of him suggests he had no more enemies than the average person, but on the other hand we all know somebody who might like us dead. He seems to have been something of a womaniser. Stretch the imagination a little. For the sake of the enquiry, assume that jealous husbands can even be found in North End.

'Less dramatic, perhaps. Somebody didn't love him. The obvious again. But discounting the injury to the face, which doen't amount to much, one blow. Not a maniac. Not a sadist. Probably not even a deliberate murderer. Some people die very easily. Many murderers have killed without meaning to kill. Nevertheless, it was no love-tap.

'Accepting our friend the pathologist's estimate that he's been dead for some days, somebody has been sitting on a corpse for some time. Not the most inconspicuous thing in the world. Not a thing you can pop out of sight under a cushion when the vicar calls. Assume somebody saw it. Knew it was there — wherever it was — but for reasons undisclosed hasn't mentioned the fact. A suggested line of enquiry, ladies and gentlemen. No more than that.

'The matter of transporting the body from Point A to Point B. From where it was to where it was found. Between yesterday when the grave was dug, and today when the grave-diggers returned to perform the finishing touches. You can't tuck a corpse under your arm. You can't cart it around in your pocket. Unless you're exceptionally well endowed with muscle you can't carry it any distance without risking hernia. Two, then. At least two. A vehicle of some sort. The possibilities — the *probabilities* — suggest that a secret has been shared. Once shared, it ceases to be a secret.'

Corn in Egypt. Or, if you like, the Lord helps those who help themselves. Reg Innes, who knew little about Egypt and even less about the Deity, might have put it another way. There's one born every minute, and *he'd* found his quota for that day. Things had started to look promising when he'd found the transom window of the ground-floor bog partly open. Five minutes later, he'd been inside searching for goodies. A bit of jewellery here, a gold hunter there, some loose change, a flash-looking cigarette lighter, a few fivers held together by an elastic band. Then he'd spotted the safe.

A very nice little safe. A Chubb, no less. And if the tele-crooks. were to be believed, it was going to be as easy as opening a tin of sardines. Just lean one ear against the door, twiddle the knobs, turn the handles then nod knowingly when the door swung open to reveal a king's ransom. But he hadn't known what the hell he was listening *for*. Come to that, he hadn't heard a damn thing. Nor, come to think of it, was it all *that* clever wandering from room to room in somebody else's house switching lights on and off. Something else the loonies on the box did all wrong.

He'd stepped back and glared at the safe. Then slowly, gradually, a truth had dawned.

A flash safe. Window-dressing. What else? 'Honest Joe Lumb' hadn't made his pile by being stupid. Income tax officers come snooping round. They examine the books. Okay, they're satisfied.

why shouldn't they be satisfied? The books they see have been carefully cooked to *make* them satisfied. They see the safe. Such a nice safe; such a strong safe. They say, 'I see you have a safe, there.' 'Sure,' says Joe. 'We'd like to look inside,' they say. 'Why not?' says Joe. And why not indeed? The safe is like the books. A con to keep government snoopers happy. Something to make them feel good and look efficient. There's not a damn thing in the safe they *shouldn't* see.

The truth had dawned, and Innes had grinned with delight at his own acumen.

Some ten minutes later, he'd prowled up the stairs and in the ceiling of the landing, he'd seen the trap-door leading to the false roof. Where else? North End thinking. North End mentality. The natural mentality of 'Honest Joe Lumb'.

A table. A chair on top of the table. A quick heave, and there'd even been a light switch and an unshaded bulb. Lots of lagging, lots of pipes, lots of wires, lots of boards and lots of junk. but behind a battered tin chest under a pile of old and soiled curtains, three carefully corded biscuit tins.

He almost held his breath as he worked at the cord holding the lid on the first tin. He almost fainted with sheer pleasure when, at last, he clawed the lid clear. Solid with notes. All tenners. All used. *And* the second tin. The third tin, almost full; plenty to go at but packed alongside the notes was an oiled-silk package. Curiosity got the better of him. He unwrapped the package, and there was a shooter and ammunition. A very neat, very deadly-looking "black gun". That's how he mentally described it. "A black gun". A firearms expert would have recognised it as a Colt, .32, hammerless, pocket model, automatic pistol. In 1929 (the year of its manufacture) it had cost the original purchaser the ridiculously small sum of twenty dollars and fifty cents.

'Certain motions must be gone through.' Flensing was reaching the end of his briefing. 'The media people would feel cheated if we denied them the obligatory picture of plain-clothes officers, carrying clipboards and pencils and knocking on doors of innocent rate-payers. Similarly, "the search". The cemetery will be taped off, officers will be issued with wellingtons and oilskins. I merely ask that, as they trample their way through the snow,

57

they show due deference. Graves must be walked across. Walk across them slowly, and with an outward show of respect. The Dog Section? I think so. A photograph of alsatians anxious to find something — if only the nearest lamp-post — is always worth a front-page spread in the local newspaper.

'The *real* enquiry.' His tone remained the same, but nobody doubted that what was about to be said would include something over and above sardonic observation. 'Snouts. I want every known snout pumped until his throat is parched. The same with gossip. No matter how stupid or trivial. Trace it back to its source. Find out how it started. Prove it or disprove it. Whatever else, don't dismiss it. This whole town is talking. North End is bursting with speculation. Rumours. Boastings. Garden-wall chit-chat. Keep it going, ladies and gentlemen. Keep it stoked. By the nature of the killing, by the nature of the disposal of the body, by the very fact of the delay between the killing and the dumping of the body *somebody* knows *something*. People who know more than we know are making educated guesses. Start with an assumption. What should have been a secret is *not* a secret. Merely hidden. An analogy. Among all the chaff there is one grain of wheat. Our job — this enquiry — boils down to raising a wind strong enough to blow away all the chaff. *Then* we can stand back and watch the grain of wheat germinate.'

Jimmy Holmes was on the run. He didn't know it — he might even have been shocked, had that patently obvious fact been pointed out to him — because, as far as his own panic-stricken and befuddled brain was able to comprehend things, he was merely sheltering from the cold and doing what he could to bring warmth back to his shivering body.

He was surrounded by a babble of noise. Virile noise. Masculine, earthy noise. The noise of a busy transport cafe well situated on an A-road on the outskirts of the city. The rattle of cutlery and crockery. The click of dominoes as men relaxed from behind the wheel. The call of orders and the chatter of men exchanging news of weather conditions.

'What's Shap like?'

'Blocked. Last I heard they'd lost two ploughs.'

'Bugger it. I think I'll ring the depot.'

'Try the motorway.'

'Oh, aye! Fifty miles out.'

Holmes curled his fingers around the pint pot in a two-handed grip. He raised it to his lips, and the brim rattled gently against his teeth.

A chair scraped and a broad-shouldered giant wearing wind-cheater and woolen cap joined him at the table.

'Cow of a night,' growled the giant cheerfully.

'Eh? Oh!' Holmes nodded silent agreement.

As the giant lifted a plate of sausage, chips and beans, a pot of tea, knife and fork and bread and butter from a tray and arranged the meal on the table, he said, 'Which direction?'

Holmes moved his shoulders.

'East's blocked north of Scotch Corner.'

'Oh!'

The giant gulped hot tea, smacked his lips, cut into the sausage and said, 'Wouldn't like to risk the M62.'

'Er — no.'

'Bloody Pennine Motorways!' The giant chewed on the sausage.

Holmes muttered unintelligible response.

'Which way you heading?'

Holmes didn't answer.

The giant loaded his fork with chips and beans and growled, 'Driving?'

'What? Er . . . no.' Holmes seemed suddenly to be aware of what was being said. What was being implied.

The giant chewed, and said, 'I'm going south. Reading. That any good?'

'Fine.' Holmes's throat felt parched. He sipped at his tea, then repeated. 'Fine. Thanks.'

Hoyle and King were in King's office. They'd left the Murder Room after the departure of Flensing and, having each issued instructions for basic night cover within their individual fields of responsibility, had left the minor matter of details to a C.I.D. and a uniformed sergeant. They were now relaxing and evaluating their briefing.

'No questions,' observed King as he leaned backwards in the desk chair and switched on an extra bar of the electric fire.

'Not so much a briefing,' agreed Hoyle. 'More of a pep-talk.'

'More than that, surely?'

'Maybe,' admitted Hoyle, and he made the admission with some reluctance.

The two men were of an age and service. They held identical rank — one in C.I.D., one in the uniformed branch — but they worked well together. They augmented each other in their duties. Sometimes they overlapped, but the overlapping never amounted to trespass. There was mutual respect, and the respect formed the bedrock for trust and friendship. There was even off-duty friendship; an occasional foursome at a decent restaurant with their wives; the Kings had visited the Hoyle's home for drinks, a buffet meal and an evening's chat, and the visits had been reciprocated.

'The wrong way.' Hoyle pulled a chair nearer, then sprawled in it with the base of his spine not far from the chair's front edge. 'Dammit, you don't detect major crime by chasing rumours.'

'*He* does,' grinned King.

'You seek facts,' insisted Hoyle. 'You gather evidence. You don't race around after fairy tales.'

King produced cigarettes and when they were smoking said, 'We're going to busy.'

Hoyle nodded and waited.

'Split it?' said King gently. Tentatively.

'How?'

'Eight on, eight off?'

'Even Flensing can't ask for more than twelve hours a day,' agreed Hoyle.

King said, 'I'll get out of this uniform. Any snags — anything I don't think I can handle while I'm covering for you I'll give you a ring. You do the same.'

'Do we tell him?' asked Hoyle.

'If he asks. If he doesn't ask . . .' King shrugged.

'Agreed.' Hoyle nodded. 'Just leave me a good paper expert while you're off duty.'

'And you leave me a good C.I.D. man to guide me round the potholes.' King drew on the cigarette, then added, 'You've been with it most of the day. I'll nip home and change. Take over at ten. You relieve me at six for the next eight hours.'

'All clever stuff,' murmured Hoyle.

'If you don't approve. If you think . . .'

'Oh, I approve,' smiled Hoyle. 'I think it's a good idea. But will *Flensing* approve?'

'If he finds out we'll soon know.'

Solly Daniels held onto his courage; gripped it there in a tight knot and refused the turbulent panic freedom enough to completely dominate his actions. He had to go somewhere. Not much, but it was his home. It could provide shelter, it could provide warmth, it could provide privacy. A man's home was his castle, right? Okay, his wasn't much of a castle, but it was *his*. The one place he might feel safe. And to stay on the streets in weather like this was plain crazy.

He walked slowly along Chamber's Court, inserted the key into the lock, pushed open the door and stepped inside.

It was the bravest thing he'd ever done in his life. He was no hero; he'd have been the first in line to admit that he was no hero. But if sheer grab-your-guts-and-do-it courage amounted to anything, Solly Daniels earned himself a medal as he switched on the light.

In the car parked within easy watching distance of Chamber's Court a plain clothes cop interrupted his makeshift, fish-and-chips supper to report the incidence over the radio. Solomon Daniels had returned home.

Probably because Charlie Beat was his personal responsibility. Probably beacause he'd suffered so much misery watching the house. Probably because the idea of being even a small cog in a murder-hunt machine made him feel he had to do *something*.

For whatever reason — and probably it was a combination of all those reasons, plus — Adamson figured a chat with Tich Cutter would do no harm. Flensing wanted rumours. Okay, Flensing could have rumours. Cutter was a great little rumour-monger. Cutter was the repository and passer-on of every rumour in North End. So, Police Constable Adamson talked with Tich Cutter.

The damn room stank to the high heavens of dog. Two whippets were curled and snuggled up to each other for warmth on a battered armchair alongside the hearth; they sniffed a little and watched Adamson with slow-blinking eyes. It was the only armchair in the room, and nobody made any move to shift them.

'Sammy Gatling,' said Adamson.

'Aye. What about him?'

Like so many small men, Cutter had a permanent air of aggression. As if forever conscious of his lack of height and ready to tear into anybody who might think he was less than a complete man.

'You'll have heard. He's been murdered.'

'Aye. What am I supposed to do?'

Ma Cutter watched the exchange. A huge woman, as suspicious and aggressive as her husband. She seemed to be standing guard over the whipper-snapper man of hers; an angry dragon — grubby and slovenly — protecting problematic treasure from the would-be spoilers.

'Any idea why he might have been murdered?'

'Who? Me?' Cutter's eyes sparked rising indignation.

'There has to be a reason,' said Adamson gently.

Tickling trout. Years back, before May had arrived, Adamson and Kath had taken a farmhouse holiday. One of those holidays you never forget. Down south in Devon. A glorious, late-summer break. And this old boy hadn't known Adamson was a cop. Very friendly, very happy, very wise in the ways of nature. He'd shown them how trout could be tickled and caught. Real rustic magic. So slow. So gossamer gentle. That's what it was like easing information — easing an opinion — from Cutter.

Adamson smiled and said, 'We've no leads.'

'So?'

'Somebody might not have liked him. It's a possibility.'

'Aye.'

It wasn't a question. It was a little more than an observation. It even bordered upon an agreement. Possibly — just *possibly* — more than a mere agreement. Tickling trout. Adamson allowed the gentle disturbance of the water to quieten, then approached from another direction.

He said, 'You serve at The Bunch of Grapes, Saturday nights.'

Cutter nodded; a single, reluctant movement of the head.

'Gatling was there.'

'He always is.'

'With Solly Daniels and Jimmy Holmes.'

'No.' Cutter paused, then muttered, 'With Jumbo Jakeman.'

Later, when telling of this question-and-answer session,

Adamson would swear that that was the moment when he first caught a glimpse of what might be gold. An exaggeration, of course. It was merely an unexpected reply. He'd seen Gatling, Daniels, Holmes and Innes arrive at Daniels's home. He knew them to be customers of The Bunch of Grapes. He'd jumped to a wrong conclusion. Nevertheless, the next question followed quite naturally.

'They were friends, were they?'

'Who?'

'Gatling and Jakeman?'

'Bobby Adamson.' Ma Cutter spoke before her husband could reply. The voice was hard and harsh. The voice of a harridan — the sort of voice he'd heard a score of times in Hunslet as a boy — and yet there seemed to be an attempt at reasonableness. Not friendship. But on the other hand, not the naked enmity he'd expected. She asked, 'Why come to Tim?'

'To ask questions,' he fenced politely.

'Why should *he* know owt?'

'Mrs Cutter.' Adamson met her half-way. More than half-way. She was a terrible woman when roused, and he was aware of this. But as he already knew, she had reason for her fury. She was caught in the rat-trap of poverty and helplessness. The only thing she had left was what she called her "pride" and because of what she was and how she'd been brought up that "pride" demanded that she be a holy terror, if only to give proof of her own existence. In the past he'd known other such women. Her attempt at reasonableness was no small effort. In a carefully modulated voice, he said, 'Mrs Cutter, we don't know where to start looking. It's a murder enquiry. Very serious.'

'He'll not be mourned.'

Adamson allowed the observation to go apparently unnoticed, and continued, 'Mr Cutter's lived here all his life. He knows more about North End — this part of North End — than I do. Who better to ask for help?'

'We're not on the same side.' It was a simple statement of fact. Not even a challenge.

'No,' said Adamson slowly, 'we're not on the same side.' He paused, then added, 'But if somebody killed Mr Cutter, I'd be asking questions to other people. Other people not on the same side.'

There was a silence, while she digested and accepted the logic. Then she said, 'You've been stood out here of a night.'

Adamson nodded.

'Not in uniform.'

'In plain clothes,' agreed Adamson.

'Watching.'

Again Adamson nodded.

'Watching what?'

Tickling trout. He was getting closer. Almost there. A movement was necessary, but the wrong movement would ruin everything.

He took a calculated risk and in a gentle voice said, 'I was watching this house, Mrs Cutter.'

'Why?' And some of the reasonableness disappeared.

'I don't know,' said Adamson truthfully. 'I was told to watch this house. Watch the comings and goings of your husband. I obey orders.'

'You must have some idea why . . .'

'No.' Adamson shook his head. Calmly. Without pushing things too far. 'An order from a sergeant. I expressed an opinion. That Mr Cutter wasn't doing anything to merit observations. That's as far as I could go. After that, I had to obey orders.'

It might have been a smile. It was certainly a movement of the lips. Not quite contempt, but not far from contempt. But with the movement of the lips some of the reasonableness returned. That, plus a hint of triumph.

She said, 'How do *you* know?'

'What?'

'That he's not up to summat?'

'I don't know,' admitted Adamson. He smiled, and added, 'It was an educated guess.'

'Oh, aye?'

'The snouts would have been around,' amplified Adamson.

'That I believe.' She returned the smile, but the contempt was still there. Contempt for Adamson? Contempt for snouts? It was hard to decide. 'That I *do* believe. And now you want Tim to turn snout.'

'If *he'd* been murdered . . .'

'All right!' For a moment the flash of anger worried Adamson. He thought he'd lost; thought the trout had flicked its tail and

64

escaped. But Ma Cutter had lost, and it was the knowledge of having lost which had triggered the burst of self-disgust. Then in a quieter tone — in a tone laced with strange but slight approval — she said, 'All right. *You* don't really belong to *them*, bobby Adamson.'

He knew what she meant. Excactly what she meant. Like believing she was recognising like. But she was wrong.

He smiled, shook his head slowly, and murmured, 'No. Not any more.'

'Happen.' She wasn't convinced. She looked at her husband and said, 'Right, tell him. If you know owt, tell him.'

Out of context it could have been the format for a situation comedy. The huge wife dominating the pygmy husband; the dragon and the mouse. It wasn't *quite* like that. In effect, Adamson had submitted himself to a test and had passed it. He was to be trusted as far as any North Ender would ever trust anybody.

And Tich Cutter knew his neighbours. Not for nothing did he lounge at street corners passing the time of day and exchanging the names of possible winners with his cronies. Little went on that Cutter didn't get wind of. And Sammy Gatling? Thick — thick as two short planks — but had a way with the ladies. Maybe because he *was* thick. 'Some of the women around here. Word gets around and they want a taste, see?' That bluntly — that crudely — being the gist of it. Sammy Gatling had been something of an experience, and him being a little soft in the head had added peculiar spice to that experience.

Ma Cutter muttered, 'Right slags, some of 'em.'

'Married women?' Adamson asked the question of Cutter.

'Married, single, owt! The only bloody thing Gatling could be proud of, so he'd shared it around. With anybody, see? Five to his own woman. God only knew how many other little brats were running the streets as a result of his antics. How many abortions the back-street biddies had performed as a spin-off to his goings on.'

'Abortions?'

'Aye.' Cutter nodded, then lowered his eyes.

'Come on,' encouraged Adamson. 'There's something else.'

'Just rumour.'

'That's what I'm after.'

'It'll not . . .'

'It *might*.'

'Jakeman,' mumbled Cutter reluctantly. 'Y'know Jakeman?'

'Jumbo Jakeman. Yes.'

'Him and Gatling. And Manford's lass.'

'Go on.'

'Well . . . she wanted rid.'

'Gatling's child?'

'Course.'

'And?'

'Jakeman gave her some stuff. Gave Gatling some stuff to give to her.'

'And?' It was a little like dragging rusted nails from old timber one at a time.

Cutter moistened his lips, glanced at his wife and muttered, 'It didn't work. It killed her.'

'Go on.'

'That's — that's all.'

'That's *not* all,' said Ma Cutter.

'It's all I know. All I've heard. I don't even know *that*, for sure.'

'Mrs Cutter?' said Adamson gently.

Quite calmly, Ma Cutter said, 'Elsie Manford "went away". That's what they said. That's the story they put around. Her father was inside. G.B.H.'

'Three years ago. Thereabouts.'

'Aye. He's out now. Been almost a year. His wife's back with him. At the time . . .'

'*We don't know.*' Cutter almost moaned the words.

'We know as much as anybody knows.' The woman wouldn't be silenced. She'd decided. Adamson could be trusted. 'Like hell the poor lass "went away". She was dead. She was got rid of. Her mother was tarting around with this other bloke. She didn't want a fuss. Didn't want Manford to know. Hush it up, see?'

'Gatling?' Adamson's throat was dry. He cleared it, then added, 'Jakeman?'

'They gave her the stuff to get rid of the bairn. Gatling was responsible. If Manford's found out . . .' She left the sentence unfinished, and added, 'Whatever he is, he was fond of that lass of his.'

The blowers and the ploughs had created walls of snow on both sides of the dual carriageway; great canyons of white walls between which the eight-wheeler roared and hissed. Inside the cab was warm and cosy with a faint smell of oil. The radio was turned down to give a soft backdrop of all-night small-talk and pop music; a sort of pastel sound contrasting with the harsh reality picked out by the great beams.

Holmes had switched himself off. He was safely encased within a steel castle; a tiny world wherein nothing could reach him; a protective capsule, part of a gigantic machine which could combat the cold and carry him away from the time and place of the nightmare. The trick was to live for the moment. No past, no future. Only *now*.

Without taking his eyes from the road ahead, the driver said, 'Comfortable?'

'Fine,' said Holmes. 'Lovely.'

Adamson finished cleaning his teeth, screwed the top back onto the tube and pulled the light-cord as he left the bathroom. He crossed the landing and entered the bedroom. He didn't need light; the wash from the street-lamp gave enough illumination. Instead of climing into bed, he paused and stared out at the snow-heavy bushes and rooftops; at the frost patterns already forming on the outside of the panes.

'Not tired?' Kath had already bathed and had been in bed almost thirty minutes.

'Tired enough,' said Adamson flatly. He turned from the window and gazed at the dim outline of his wife's face on the pillow. In a gentle tone — speaking the words delicately, as if rough handling might shatter them — he said, 'I think I've detected the murder.'

'You've . . .' She pushed herself into a sitting position. 'You mean you've . . .'

'Listen to me, Kath.' There was a pleading and a quiet desperation in his tone. He stepped from the window and sat on the edge of the bed. He clasped one of her hands as he said, 'I need help. I need advice. I need *your* advice, pet.'

She listened as he told her. She listened without interrupting, and he told her without frills and without exaggeration. He told her the "what", the "how" and the "why", and it was the "why" that worried him.

He ended, 'That's why they coughed luv. Because it was *me*. Because Ma Cutter recognised her own kind. Hunslet, see? A lout. Somebody like *them*. As if — as if I'd a sign hanging round my neck.'

'That's not true.' She squeezed his hand. 'You're a good man, Peter. A good husband, a good father. It doesn't matter where you were born.'

'It matters,' he breathed.

'A good policeman,' she continued. 'They trust you . . .'

'Because . . .'

'. . . . because you're a good policeman. Don't sell yourself short, darling. I wouldn't have married a lout. I wouldn't have allowed a lout to be the father of our daughter.'

He held onto her hand as if drowning and croaked, 'I don't often say it. I should say it more often. Every day.'

'What?'

'How lucky I am. How much I love you.'

In the dim light he could see her smile.

'No need,' she said gently. 'You *show* me. Every day. Every hour. *I'm* the lucky one.'

He raised her hand to his lips. Held it there, then lowered it.

He sighed, and said, 'I'd better get dressed. Get down to the station. Let them know about the . . .'

'No.'

'Kath, pet, it's important. Murder. I have to . . .'

'You didn't go straight to the station,' she reminded him. 'You came home. Had a bath. You were coming to bed.'

'I was a bit . . .' He searched for the words. 'A bit unsure. A bit shaken.'

'But now you're sure?'

'Aye. Thanks to you.'

'It might mean staying on duty all night.'

'Not much doubt.'

'It won't make him any less dead. Gatling.' There was the barest hint of coquettishness in her tone. 'It's detected. It'll still be detected. It won't make a scrap of difference.'

'I know. But . . .'

'Peter, darling, I think you should come to bed. I think you've been on duty long enough for one day. I think you should come to bed. I think we should make love. Then I think you should have a good night's sleep.' She smiled and added, 'You asked my advice.'

'Aye.'

'That's my advice.'

THREE

Detective Sergeant Andrew Ballester didn't go for all the cigarette-smoking-is-injurious-to-health eyewash. He was a two-before-breakfast man, and had the cough to prove it. One while shaving; dexterously switching electric razor and cigarette from hand to hand while he contorted his face in order that the blades might run against the grain of the stubble. One when he'd reached the kitchen and while he waited for the kettle to boil.

He was well into his second cigarette, the kettle had started to hiss and, gradually, his mental alertness was rising to a point where (as always) he wished life hadn't kicked him in the crotch quite so hard and quite so often. He wished, for example, his wife hadn't done the dirty on him or, if she'd *had* to, that the circumstances hadn't had the touch of a third-rate comedian telling a mucky joke. The milkman, for Christ's sake! Had it been a parson, had it been a fellow-copper, had it been just about *anybody*. But the bloody milkman. Real seaside postcard stuff, and he hadn't been amused. He *still* wasn't amused. Just let him get his fingers within reaching distance of that milkman's throat . . .

Not that he missed his wife, you understand. The old biddie across the street popped in three afternoons a week and shifted the dust from Point A to Point B, and that was about all his missus had ever done. But that wasn't the point. If a wife left her husband, there had to be a reason. Some bloke loaded to the gills with loot. Some lounge lizard with a smooth line of patter. Some lying hound promising everlasting exoticism on sun-drenched beaches. Something! But a bloody *milkman*.

This line of reasoning always accompanied the second cigarette. He'd lived alone for less than a year and he hadn't yet grown used to the idea. He hadn't yet considered the possibility that *he* might have been at fault; that even a humble milk roundsman might offer something he'd never thought of offering.

In kindness, and by stretching excuses to near-snapping-point, it might be said that Ballester lived for his work; that being a

73

copper was, for him, a twenty-four-hours-a-day-seven-days-a-week job. And that, that being the case, he'd been a fool for taking a wife in the first place. He often kidded himself enough to grab a crumb of comfort from that thought. On the other hand, and equally often, he recognised that comfort as so much crap.

The kettle began to boil and splutter. He fished two tea bags from a caddy, dropped them into a brown, pot-bellied teapot, switched off the elctricity and poured boiling water over the tea bags.

The cigarette was almost finished. He opened the door leading to the rear garden and, as the chill air caught his throat he grabbed what was left of the cigarette from his lips, tossed it into the snow-covered lawn and folded in a bout of hawking and coughing.

Stinking weather. He'd been up till well past midnight in the living quarters of his favourite boozer. Some hair-splitting miffs might have called it after-hours drinking. Strictly speaking, maybe; he'd paid his corner. But he'd been *working*. Whatever else, he'd been doing what he was paid to do. Flensing had said 'ask around'. That's what he'd been doing. Asking around. Harry Peel, the landlord, didn't miss much. Nor did his wife, Edna. All the chat from the boozer, see? All the nudge-nudge wink-wink stuff. A few pints at the same time, but what was that? All the pub talk since they'd found Gatling's body. All the speculation. Ninety per cent of it cobblers, of course it was. But — y'know — maybe . . .

I mean *why* pick Fred Kelly's grave? It was a question. A fair, legitimate question. Kelly hadn't been too popular. Nor, come to that, had Gatling. The stiff had been dead for a day or two. Been kept above ground for *something*. Kelly'd been snuffing it. Common knowledge. Any day now. Any minute. Supposing somebody *had* wanted to screw Kelly, even after he was dead. Somebody who didn't like Gatling any more than he liked Kelly. The North Enders were mad sods. Every last one of 'em. It was possible. Quite possible. Even *likely*.

Ballester recovered his breath, bent to pick up the morning milk . . . and immediately remembered a certain milkman.

The copper covering Charlie Beat while Adamson was absent on murder enquiries was one of the young bloods of the force.

Bearded — the officer Solly had seen standing at the entrance of the Albion Bingo Hall — and, when not in uniform, one of the lads of the village. His was a life-style which a few years before would have earned him the swift boot from any constabulary in the United Kingdom. Marriage was strictly for the stone-age people; the honest thing (the *natural* thing) was to have a personal pad, with a chick installed as part of the fittings on a strict when-either-of-us-gets-bored-you-blow basis. Off-duty means just that. *Off*-duty. You dressed the way you wanted to dress, the disco was a second home and a little pot-smoking on the quiet hurt nobody. Jesus, this come-along-a-me image was strictly for the dodo. This was just a job, man. A means of earning good bread. All this "vocational" crap was for creeps short on marbles. The world went round — one spin every day — and you kept with it, otherwise you were missing out on the really important things.

Take this dump; this Chamber's Court thing. Jesus H. Christ! People didn't *live* here. No self-respecting dog would live in a crummy spot like this. They *existed*. Cave-dwelling stuff, kid. Raw bones and rabbit skins. Nobody with any . . .

He interrupted his personal cogitations long enough to twitch his nose. The face foliage formed a natural sieve, nevertheless there was a distinct hint of gas. A *distinct* hint. He followed the smell and ended up at the door. He unhitched his personal radio, pressed the transmit button and uttered words which, in the course of time, were to become a classical example of how *not* to report an incident.

'Hey man. The Gas Board seem to have dropped another goolie.'

He released the button, and a slightly tinny version of Sergeant Lowe's voice said, 'Who the hell *is* that? And what sort of crap-arsed radio procedure is *that* supposed to be?'

Lowe's snarl had the desired effect. An approximation of sanity was established and, in little more than ten minutes, Sergeant Lowe joined the bearded wonder in Chamber's Court.

'Kick the door in,' said Lowe.

'Hey, man, we can't . . .'

'I'm not asking for a show of bloody hands,' exploded Lowe. 'Just for once in your useless life do what you're *told* to do. Get that damn door open.' Then, as an afterthought, 'And, if you're thinking of striking matches, give me a hundred yards start.'

Solly was dead. Long dead and stiffening. His head was in the oven against which Sammy Gatling had fallen. He'd removed the shelves and rested his check upon a none-too-clean cushion. The cushion had been further stained by the tiny discharge from his mouth as the gas had moved into its final phase of deadly efficiency.

The doors and windows were opened. Lowe held a handkerchief to his face as he dragged the corpse out of the room and into the street. The bearded copper thought he was helping, as he held the oven steady. Maybe he was helping, but he was also handling and destroying what evidence there was via which forensic scientists might have linked the base of Sammy Gatling's skull with a corner of the oven.

Hallsworth Hill Divisional C.I.D. Office. Take a C.I.D. Office — *any* C.I.D. Office — and you have almost every C.I.D. Office in the land. Rows of chipped and untidy desks; swivel-chairs that won't swivel; steel filing cabinets that won't lock; fly-blown calendars showing scantily-clad females of impossible proportions risking a double-hernia in an attempt to hold soft-porn poses; typewriters that sometimes work, but more often don't; ash-trays overspilling with spent matches and dog-ends; an overall colour scheme of pastel puke. All this, and untidy chaos beyond belief.

Hallsworth Hill Divisional C.I.D. Office.

The two jacks — both world-weary detective constables — were discussing the previous night's break-in.

'Something wrong,' mused the first D.C.

'What?'

'Watches, a handful of jewellery, a few loose quid. The whole lot worth five hundred. No more. All that weeping and wailing.'

'Five hundred's five hundred, mate.'

'It's insured.'

'So?'

'He runs two cars. An Aston Martin and a Ford Cortina for his wife to go shopping in. With what *he's* got, plus my next month's cheque, I'd be a millionaire.'

The second D.C. moved his shoulders and said, 'Having your house bust. It's a traumatic experience.'

'Yeah. So the text books say.'

'Bound to be.'

'He's a bookie, old son. The first requisite. Cauterised nerves.'

'You think he's on the fiddle?'

'I *know* he's on the fiddle. I can feel it in my water.'

'Stuff nicked he hasn't mentioned?'

'What else?'

'We'll soon know.' The second D.C. moved his bum; the radiator was becoming too warm for comfort. 'Reg Innes. The pilluck left dabs all over the place. We'll ask him when he's nabbed.'

'Circulated it?'

'Sure. North End's *very* interested. Possible connection with the murder thing.'

'Innes?' The first D.C. looked mildly surprised.

'That's what they tell me.'

'That should teach him to fart in church.'

Hoyle said, 'You want me to come with you?'

'I think you should, sir.'

They were in the Murder Room. Hoyle had relieved King at six o'clock and, less than two hours later, Adamson had arrived, waited until Hoyle was obviously clear of all immediate duties, then taken the detective chief inspector to a quiet corner of the room and told him of the visit to the Cutter household and its consequences.

Hoyle had listened, and Adamson was grateful for the serious, almost respectful, manner in which this comparatively high-ranking officer had received what was, in effect, a rather doubtful angle on the enquiry into the death of Samuel Gatling.

'Assuming it's right.' Hoyle held an opened packet of cigarettes to Adamson and Adamson took one. 'Assuming there's no exaggeration. That what the Cutters say is no more than the truth.'

'I know.' Adamson held the tip of the cigarette into the proffered flame of the lighter and waited until Hoyle had lighted his own cigarette. 'A second murder.'

'Did you know the daughter? Elsie Manford?'

'No, sir.' Adamson hesitated, then said, 'Knew her by sight. Y'know, knew she was Bill Manford's daughter. But not to talk to.'

'But not recently?'

'No, sir. Like Ma Cutter said. She "went away". That was the story put around. I heard *that*. I'd no reason to doubt it. That was close on three years ago. Maybe nearer two.'

Hoyle smoked his cigarette and digested the information in silence. He was a careful man; he rarely jumped gates without checking what he might land in. Rumour. That's what it boiled down to and, for the moment, that's *all* it boiled down to. But rumour that had to be checked and followed through. Proved or disproved. It couldn't just be left. Maybe — just *maybe* — Flensing's technique sometimes worked.

'Manford?' he murmered.

'Bill Manford.' Adamson rubbed the nape of his neck. 'Bit of a wild man. *Was.*'

'Was?'

'Do they go straight, sir? Ever?' It was a sombre question, asked with a worried frown and of an expert.

'Sometimes,' said Hoyle gently. 'I've known it to happen.'

'I'd have bet my life on it,' said Adamson sadly.

'You don't *have* to be wrong.'

'A hell of a list,' sighed Adamson. 'But — y'know — he swore he'd had enough. Not bitter. Not really tamed, I suppose. Just — y'know — grown up. Grown out of it.'

More information; tiny scraps of information that had to be carefully weighed and assessed. That plus Adamson's reliability as a judge of character. This was the big 'un. Not "Do you mind telling us where you were last night, Mr Manford?" This time, "Do you mind telling us whether you murdered Samuel Gatling?" And to ask *that* brand of question something far more substantial than North End gossip was needed.

'Gatling's reputation?'

'With women?'

Hoyle nodded.

'It's North End, sir.' As far as Adamson was concerned that said everything. He amplified, 'Morals don't mean much. There aren't too many marriage licences. A woman has a kid. Very often her man thinks — *hopes* — it's his. He's not too sure, but he can't kick up much of a fuss. He's on the same game himself.'

'Quite.' Hoyle nodded part-understanding. 'But *Gatling*?'

Adamson said, 'He had a name.' A wry smile touched his lips. 'They have to be proud of *something*, sir. How true it was, I don't know. His reputation, I mean. They kiss and tell there. Sometimes they tell when they haven't kissed. Notches on the gun. That sort of thing.'

'Your patch.'

'Charlie Beat,' said Adamson heavily.

'Compared with the rest of North End?'

'The pus inside the boil,' replied Adamson bluntly.

'As bad as that?'

'I bobby it. I don't have to *like* it.'

There was something in the way it was said. Something in the tone. Something deeper than simple disgust. A strange, perspicacious quality. A recognition; an acknowledgement. Rather like a patient with an ugly disease; an acceptance of the disease and a silent rage at its ugliness. Hoyle eyed Adamson with quizzical concern for a moment.

'The wife?' he asked. 'Manford's wife?'

'Edwina?'

'Would she?'

'Cover up the murder of her own daughter?'

'That's what it amounts to.'

'Manford was a terror. *Was* at the time. Maybe still is. Yes.' Adamson nodded slowly. 'She'd do it. Self-preservation. If *she* was tooling around with other men. If she thought Manford might find out. She'd cover up.' He paused, then added, 'They all would.'

Hoyle smoked his cigarette meditatively for a few moments. Thought was needed. Thought and care. Knitting fog was bulldozer work by comparison. Without being told he knew the Civil Liberties crowd there slavering on the side-lines, watching with eagle eyes for some wicked policeman to utter so much as a single naughty word to one of the whiter-than-white little innocents of North End. In God's name *why*? Somebody had to be asked questions and, if necessary, made to answer them. In the final act somebody had to be accused. *Somebody* had killed Gatling.

He asked, 'Manford? Does he work?'

'For the local water authority. Labouring. I'm told he has a good work record.'

'So he'll be at work today?'

'Yes, sir.'

'His wife?'

'She works evenings behind the bar of The Bunch of Grapes.'

'Ah!'

'Yes, sir,' murmured Adamson. 'Cutter works alongside her Saturday evenings. That's one reason why it might not be hot air.'

'You mean she might have confided in Cutter?'

'I doubt it.' Adamson twisted his lips. '*Nobody* confides in Tich Cutter. Might as well broadcast it on the local radio.'

'Nevertheless . . .' Hoyle left the sentence unfinished.

Adamson moved his cigarette in a tiny gesture of mild disgust as he said, 'It's a pub. Customers. They talk. Barmaids. It's not all one-way traffic. *She* might have wanted a shoulder to cry on. Then whisper of it got back to Cutter. God knows how these things go. They brag and boast a lot. All of 'em.'

'Started your notebook for today?' Hoyle sounded businesslike; as if he'd reached a firm decision.

'No, sir.'

'Start it.' Hoyle made a movement towards the sergeant handling the Murder Log. 'We'll start with The Bunch of Grapes.'

Adamson took his notebook from his inside pocket and wrote — *Thursday, 17th December*.

Innes had only been to the Big City once in his life. A Cup Final; one of a crowd of cronies; never completely sober from leaving the train; hell-raising before the match, during the match and after the match; storming through Soho and being fleeced by clip-joint operators to whom they were hicks there for the taking. Innes wasn't too keen on London. It was bigger than Lessford. Much bigger. It was even bigger than Leeds.

Too big. Too many strangers. Too many damn blacks.

Innes had the mentality of his kind. He was white which, by simple definition, meant he was superior to all non-whites. He was English, ergo he had a head start on every non-English man, woman and child in the world, whatever their colour. The rest were "Froggies", "Krauts", "Spicks", "Kykes", "Yanks",

"Wogs" and a score of other names. If the skin pigmentation moved beyond a certain distance from his own they were "Nignogs". That simple and that stupid. Sir Garfield Sobers was one of the greatest cricketers ever to grace a cricket field, but as far as Innes was concerned he was a nig-nog. Einstein had a brain and a humility capable of causing ordinary men to stand in wide-eyed wonder, but to Innes he was a kyke. It was a belief amounting to a religion. A fanaticism. And yet, despite this "superiority", he was vaguely frightened of them. They worried him because they were not of his breed. They couldn't be trusted. They were enemies by reason of their skin.

He humped the zip-topped hold-all out of King's Cross Station and wandered around the streets and squares of the district. Hotels galore. Guest houses. Some slicked up a little. Others with paint peeling and colour-wash flaking. In some streets even the air of tatty respectability had been thrown overboard.

But Innes wanted a bed. He had to *have* a bed. He was knackered. He needed sleep. The night journey south hadn't been easy. Other people in the compartment; people he didn't know; people who *might* have been cat-napping but who might *not* have been cat-napping; people who might have been waiting to slip the hold-all from between his legs. No knowing. You couldn't trust a bloody soul. Not if you'd any sense. Not if you were carting this much money around.

'How much? He daren't think. He daren't contemplate. He hadn't yet had chance to count it; just a few notes stuffed into an inside pocket for immediate use, then the rest rammed tight in the hold-all. Thousands, that for sure. Tens of thousands. Maybe *hundreds* of thousands. Christ, he'd never have to work or worry again. Just somewhere temporary. That's all he needed. Somewhere to sleep then, having slept, somewhere to think. What to do? Where to put it? Where to *go*?

Jesus, Joseph and Mary! All his life he'd wanted money. A fortune. The good life; booze, birds and all the other luxuries the T.V. ads promised if the cabbage patch was big enough. Okay, now he had it. He *had* it. And he *still* had problems. Where to sleep and what to do *with* it?

He turned from the snow-cleared pavement, climbed the half-dozen shallow steps and thumbed a bell-push.

What the hell? Anywhere. Just a room with a bed and a door

81

with a lock. That's what he needed. That's *all* he needed.

To concertina time a little.

The Forensic Science Lab — the so-called "test-tube babies" — earned a grain or two of corn. They examined the sheet. Via their own brand of magic they came up with enough of a laundry-mark to send a D.C. on enquiries. The laundry kept good records; the sheet had originally been part of the bed-linen of a now defunct fever hospital. More enquiries. Most of the bed-linen (including all the sheets) had been sold as a job lot to a private old people's home. 'Thank you, sir. That's a big help.' 'Ma'am, some few years ago — about seven years ago — you bought some sheets from a fever hospital . . .' 'Vicar, I wonder if you remember. A couple of years back, you had a jumble sale. You had some second-hand sheetes given from . . .' 'Missus, can you help me, please? Two years ago, at the church jumble sale, you were on one of the stalls. You had some sheets. Would it be possible to tell me . . .'

'That's it then, sir,' reported the D.C. triumphantly. 'Solly Daniels bought two at a jumble sale. We've traced where the murder was committed.'

The hooded eyes stared at him disconcertingly for a moment, then Flensing said, 'Not by a few leagues, my eager young friend. Trot off and do some more enquiries. Come back, tell me where every other sheet from the fever hospital is, then tell me we know Gatling was wrapped in one of the sheets bought by Daniels. I'll tend to believe you. I'll be prepared to accept the possibility that we know where a body was parcelled up for delivery. Not, necessarily, where Gatling was killed.'

But that can only be told by concertinaring time.

Ethel Kelly really was fed up with this damn husband of hers. In life he'd been a continual nuisance and even now, in death, he was being as awkward as the very devil. Why wouldn't he be buried decent, like any normal, law-abiding corpse? First some other fool body had jumped the queue to the grave, now within hours of an encore, this noisy, bombastic detective sergeant was tearing the scabs from old sores and doing his best to ruin a second attempt at a nice send off.

'How do I know whether he knew Gatling or not?' she

snapped. 'He had *his* friends, I had *mine*. We hadn't a lot in common.'

'He was your husband.'

'Big deal!'

'I'm damned if I can see how . . .' Ballester suddenly remembered a certain milkman and "saw how" with blinding clarity. He closed his mouth, then in a quieter tone said, 'You'll know *some* of the people he knew?'

'Some of 'em,' she admitted with a certain primness.

'For instance?'

'He had some very funny friends.'

'Funny?'

'"Disgusting" is a better word.'

'Oh, aye?'

'*I* wouldn't have had them as friends.'

'For instance?' repeated Ballester.

'Murphy.'

'Murphy?'

'Spud Murphy. What on earth anybody sees in *him* I'll never know.'

'It takes all sorts,' murmured Ballester.

'So they tell me. Personally, I can't see how *that* sort's needed.'

'Do you know his address?'

'If you could *call* it an address.'

Clarence Quince. That was the name on the board above the main entrance and, after the name, came the usual guff about "intoxicating liquor", "music singing and dancing" and "on and off the premises".

Clary Quince was ridiculously proud of that board. It gave him status; in an immediate world stiff with hooks and felons he could glance up at that board and take comfort from the fact that *he* was different. That name wouldn't be there, otherwise. *He* wasn't a criminal. Or, to be more precise, *he* hadn't been caught with his pants round his ankles.

He was "mine host". That's how he figured himself . . . as "mine host". It was an excellent excuse. It gave him a reason for spending most of his time on the customer's side of the bar, drumming up trade and supping free beer, while his wife, Con, worked her tits off pulling pints, serving shorts and giving the clients wrong change whenever she thought she could get away with it. Ask Clary Quince what sort of a house The Bunch of Grapes was and he wouldn't hesitate in his answer. 'A homely house. An inn with old world character.' In North End, for Christ's sake! (He'd read it in an advert for holidays in Scotland and he'd learned it by heart.) And yet he'd grown to believe it — he'd said it enough times to convince himself — and he would have been hurt and offended had somebody reminded him that the only "old world" thing about The Bunch of Grapes was the old world muck.

He was a short man — no taller than Tich Cutter — but, unlike Cutter, heavy boned and with a congenital twist of the spine which forced him to hold himself slightly lop-sided, as if he was forever walking along the side of a hill. He was stocky, hard-muscled and square jawed, and the back-slapping bonhomie he displayed to his customers was as false as greasepaint.

At the moment he was tieless, with the sleeves of his shirt rolled above the elbows, and was wearing tattered, zip-up slippers, baggy flannel trousers and a stained waistcoat. He hadn't yet shaved and the stubble on his cheeks, chin and neck showed more than a fair share of grey, which was matched by the wildness of his uncombed hair.

'She helps the wife behind the bar,' he said, and it was obvious that he was playing for time in which to think.

'Therefore, you know her,' said Hoyle patiently.

'Aye.' Quince slopped his way behind the bar, uncovered the pumps and pulled himself his first drink of the day, as he continued, 'She doesn't twist. At least, she doesn't twist *me*. That's all *I* ask.'

'She has a daughter,' said Hoyle gently.

'Aye. Elsie. Elsie Manford.'

'Has? Or *had*?'

'Sorry?' Quince tasted the newly drawn beer and sucked his lips.

'Gatling's been killed.' Hoyle progressed slowly. Carefully. 'Murdered.'

Quince waited.

'Any connection?' asked Hoyle. 'Obvious connection? *Rumoured* connection?'

'Between Edwina Manford and . . .'

84

'No. *Elsie* Manford.'

'Oh, aye?'

'Does that mean there is or there isn't?'

'What?' Quince tasted the beer again.

'Stop farting around, Quince.' Adamson spoke for the first time. He wasn't C.I.D. He was a common-or-garden copper and all this dodging and weaving wasn't something he went in for. Ask a question, get an answer or else ... That was the only language Charlie Beat scum understood. He growled, 'This place. I'll haunt it, if that's what you're after. You'll cover those pumps on time. On the button. Not so much as a packet of crisps after hours. That what you want?'

'Is he threatening me?' Quince asked Hoyle the question.

'Is he?' Hoyle threw the question back with a disarming smile.

'Sounds like it.'

'You should know.'

'Is he allowed?'

'You want an honest answer?'

'Aye.'

'The three of us. Just us three.' Hoyle allowed the smile to stay in position. 'Two-to-one. That's the odds. He's allowed to break your arm, if that's what it needs to get at the truth.'

Quince turned his head and bawled, '*Con*!'

A dumpy woman, still in dressing-gown and curlers, waddled sleepily from the living quarters and into the bar parlour. She stopped and stood silent.

'Altered the odds a bit.' Quince sucked some more beer from the glass.

'We could,' murmered Hoyle, 'call in half a dozen more coppers.'

'Out-play you at silly buggers,' added Adamson.

'Or — as Constable Adamson suggests — you could stop farting around. Answer some simple questions.'

Quince planted the glass of beer on the top of the counter. He turned and helped himself to a packet of cheroots and a box of matches from their display cabinet behind the bar. Slowly, deliberately, he opened the packet, took a cheroot and stripped it of its cellophane jacket.

Still watching the movements of his stained fingers, he said, 'Mash some tea, Con.'

The dumpy woman turned and retreated back into the living quarters.

Quince struck a match, held the flame to the end of the cheroot, blew smoke at the match flame, then observed, 'Edwina's anybody's meat.'

'Was? Or still is?' asked Hoyle.

'Always will be.' Quince tossed the matches and the packet of cheroots onto the bar counter and took up the beer again. With the beer in one hand and the cheroot in the other he smoked and drank as the conversation continued.

'Bill Manford's stir crazy.'

'I wouldn't say that,' contradicted Adamson.

'Would *you* know?'

'I think he's going straight.'

'Stir crazy?' Hoyle sought amplification.

'Like a punchy.' Quince moved the cheroot in a gesture of impatience at Hoyle's apparent ignorance. 'Stupid. She could shack up with anybody. He wouldn't know because his brain doesn't *want* to know.'

'And Elsie?'

'Like mother, like daughter.'

Adamson said, 'He thought a lot of that daughter.'

'So?'

'Where is she?' asked Hoyle gently.

'I heard she was up the spout.' Quince stared at the glowing end of the cheroot and added, 'That's what I heard.'

'When?'

'Just before she went away.'

'"Went away",' echoed Hoyle softly.

'Aye.' Quince continued to stare at the smouldering cheroot.

Adamson became aware of the smell of the room. The stench. Sour ale and stale tobacco smoke. When the hell were the windows last opened? When the hell was the place last *cleaned*? God, he'd known public urinals smell sweeter.

In a harsh voice he said, 'Elsie Manford was up the spout. All right. Who *put* her up the spout?'

'I wasn't there at the time,' sneered Quince.

'Look, don't start getting . . .'

'Who *claimed* to have put her up the spout?' Hoyle stepped in before it grew into a slanging match.

Quince moved his shoulders.

'Who *might* have?' teased Hoyle.

'Anybody with balls.'

'Make an educated guess,' suggested Hoyle with a smile.

Quince hesitated, then said, 'People talked about Sammy Gatling.'

'Did Sammy Gatling talk about Sammy Gatling?'

'He might have. I don't remember.'

'You're on safe ground,' rasped Adamson. 'You *don't* remember. He *can't* remember.'

Very gently Hoyle asked, 'Could Elsie Manford remember?'

Quince didn't answer. He drank beer, swallowed, then drew on the cheroot.

Quietly, slowly Hoyle said, 'Did Edwina ask *you* to arrange the abortion?'

'Eh?' Quince was as suspicious as a suddenly awakened cat.

'She worked here,' argued Hoyle remorselessly. 'She still works here. You're friends. Good friends. You know her well enough to know the state of her morals. All about her. Her daughter was pregnant. Her husband was inside. You're a smart man, Quince. A man who knows things. Knows people. A quiet little abortion before the husband gets to know. Who else would she turn to?'

'You're jumping at things.' Quince talked a little too quickly. He glanced apprehensively at the door leading to the living quarters. 'That's an accusation. You've no right . . .'

'Should we ask your wife?' asked Hoyle sweetly.

'Eh?'

'She works behind the bar. Alongside Edwina. She might have asked *her* to . . .'

'No!' Quince gulped beer. 'She doesn't know owt.'

'Y'know what?' Adamson grinned; a grin of triumph and delight. An ugly grin, in that it contained no humour. 'I think if we went to Bill Manford and told him that you and his wife were sawing a length off now and again, stir crazy or not, he'd believe us because we wouldn't be far out. Then he'd be down here and you'd end up a nasty mess in the nearest gutter. And what was left your missus would hose down the nearest drain. That's what *I* think. And I think it's a bloody good idea. It would save a lot of time.'

Quince looked first at Hoyle, then at Adamson, then, once

again, at Hoyle. On Hoyle's face he saw impassiveness; a complete repression of all feeling. In Adamson's expression he saw exultance and repulsion in an equal mix. No mercy. No hope of either of them "understanding".

He muttered, 'It's blackmail. You know *that*?'

'Aye.' Adamson nodded, grimly.

Hoyle said, 'It's more than blackmail, Quince. It's murder.'

Quince turned his head and bawled, 'Con! Don't bother with that tea.'

Strictly speaking Lowe wasn't allowed in the Murder Room. His had not been one of the names listed at that first briefing. Nevertheless, in view of the suicide of Solly Daniels, Flensing didn't press the matter. He listened as the uniformed sergeant delivered a verbal report.

'Who's handling it?' asked Flensing.

'I reckon I am,' sighed Lowe. 'The man covering Charlie Beat isn't all that . . .'

'*You* are,' interrupted Flensing flatly. 'On the face of it treat it as a Sudden Death — suicide — but as a very *special* Sudden Death. Next-of-kin?'

'Nothing, so far.' A frown touched Lowe's face. 'No Christmas cards. Nothing. The neighbours don't know anybody.'

'Don't press things. Grab a constable you can trust.'

'Ellis?' suggested Lowe.

'The character who's perfected his own Missing-from-Home system?' The hooded eyes remaing bored and expressionless, but an eyebrow lifted itself a millimetre higher.

'He's reliable, sir.'

'Have faith, brother, have faith,' murmured Flensing then, without a change of tone, 'Uniform. Both of you. Nothing to make the citizenry suspicious. Lock yourselves in, then take the house apart. Everything. All his private little fetishes. The colour of socks he favoured. The lot. When you leave that house I want you to be able to write a detailed biography of Daniels, from the date of his birth to the moment he decided to use gas he knew he wouldn't pay for. With footnotes attached. Do I make myself clear, sergeant?'

'Yes, sir.' Lowe cleared his throat. 'As I understand things, sir, he's a suspect in the Gatling case.'

'Shall we say a prospective candidate.'

'Yes, sir. In that case . . .'

'No formal identification, sergeant.'

'Eh?' Lowe gaped a little.

'He's on ice, I take it?'

'Yes, sir. In the morgue. I was hoping to . . .'

'Leave him there. He'll keep. At the Inquest we'll throw a handful of sand in the coroner's eyes. We know who he is — formal identification hasn't been made, however — with your permission we'd like to keep him on top until formal identification *is* made.'

'Will he — will he wear it?' Lowe looked uncertain.

'If it's phrased carefully. If, by implication, we suggest he might need to be dug up if he's buried too quickly. Coroners don't like gutter-press headlines. They shy away from the bare *possibililty* of gutter-press headlines. They can be manoeuvred.'

'Yes, sir. But I can't see . . .'

'Innes and Holmes,' said Flensing. 'Heard of them?'

'Yes, sir. They were with . . .'

'There's a circulation out requesting their apprehension. The usual waste of time, money and energy. Every police officer in the United Kingdom is looking for Innes and Holmes, sergeant. They'll be found . . . *if* they step smartly forward and insist upon giving themselves up. This time it would make me a happy man if they *were* searched for and found.'

'Yes, sir. I'll . . .'

'You'll light a few well-placed rockets, if you please. You'll use my name as the blue touch-paper.'

'Yes, sir.'

'Then, when they're found — either or both — we'll play at "formal identification". Without preamble. Suddenly. Unexpectedly. The reaction might be interesting.'

Kath Adamson was doing the ironing. Not for her the launderette method; the bung-'em-in-measure-the-soap-powder-press-the-button-and-wait way of dealing with the weekly wash. Clothes were very personal things. If you'd sense, you chose carefully, bought the best you could afford, then treated them with respect. Coloureds were coloureds, whites were whites, prints were prints. Cotton, nylon, wool. Good grief, each *article* of clothing needed its own individual handling. It was one of the many things being a good wife was all about. As a girl she'd been *taught* — her and her two sisters — her mother had had the patience to explain and the discipline to insist. Any fool could throw things into hot, soapy water, but that wasn't *washing* them. That wasn't *caring* for them. That wasn't being a *wife*.

Even the automatic washing machine — when Peter had insisted — she hadn't *liked*. She'd gradually become used to it, but even today she couldn't bring herself to completely trust it. It had to be watched. It had to be treated with suspicion almost amounting to disbelief.

Whereas ironing . . .

There was a warm comfortableness about ironing. Something almost creative. Clean but rumpled clothes. Then smooth and immaculately creased garments. It demanded skill. At least skill. Possibly even talent. There was an end-product; a clean and beautifully folded garment. Warm to the touch and very personal.

Like Peter. Very much like Peter.

At times like this she was a little frightened. Sometimes — just occasionally — *very* frightened. Should a woman's thoughts stray so much and so often to her man? To her husband? After so many years of married life? Was she unique? Peculiar? Or had she been touched by the Gods? It was something she daren't ask any of her friends. It was too private a thing. Not like babies and having babies; much, much more private than *that*. Too private even to mention to Peter himself.

Last night, for example. At *their* age, and with a teenage daughter in the next bedroom. But it hadn't been wrong. It hadn't even been carnal. Merely vital and very necessary. *Very* necessary.

She could read his thoughts. Truly . . . she could read his thoughts. Know what he was going to say — almost the very words he'd use — before he said them. She could feel his emotions, as strongly and as surely as if they were her own. That was the measure of their closeness. That she knew what he was thinking, even when he was silent. Even when he didn't *say* anything.

Again last night . . .

Hunslet. The cross he would carry to the grave. His everlasting burden. That he'd been born and lived his formative years in

90

Hunslet. Dear Peter. Poor Peter. As if it mattered. But it did matter to him. To him it would *always* matter.

She knew. He spoke of it rarely — these days hardly at all — but it was there, and she knew.

Years ago when they'd first met — when they'd first realised that something special was happening — he'd taken her there. A couple of times. To meet his parents, to meet his family. Coyly. As if embarrassed by the place of his birth, and the place where his kin still lived. She'd gone, she'd met them and she'd said little. But she'd remember that place — that Hunslet — for the rest of her life.

The atmosphere. Not just the filth; the dinginess; the canyon after canyon of cobbled streets with close-packed, back-to-back terrace houses. Not just the dirt, the decades of accumulated grime. That was nothing. That couldn't be helped. That was merely an evil legacy of the Industrial Revolution. But the *atmosphere*. The hatred, the bitterness, the bigotry. The monstrous deformity of mind; the refusal to accept reasons, or excuses, or even some degree of moderation. There was an air of destruction about the place; self-destruction and blind anarchy.

And Peter had come from this place. *Her* Peter. The kindest and most complete man she'd ever known.

But with this invisible chip on his shoulder. The "Hunslet" chip. One reason why he bathed twice a day. Every day. Even when he'd been ill — running a raging temperature and ordered to stay in bed by the medic — dragging himself to the bathroom, twice every day, to soap and scrub. To rid himself of what he believed was unseen "dirt".

As with his love-making. So gentle. So tentative. Almost apologetic. Then, so violent; so savage; so wild. Like last night . . . so *complete*. Followed by the almost shame-faced apology. 'I'm sorry, pet. I'm sorry.'

Sorry! The one thing she could forgive Hunslet for if, indeed, Hunslet was the basic trigger for his explosion of passion. That every woman might have a man to whom she meant so much; that every woman might be so *sure* of her husband.

She ran the tips of her fingers across the surface of the shirt she'd just finished ironing. So warm, so clean, so personal. She smiled at her memories.

Holmes was in Birmingham. How the hell he'd arrived at Birmingham he didn't rightly know. The original lift had been to Reading, but there'd been another pull-in — a short break in the small hours — and the driver had asked questions.

'You sure you're not on the run, mate?'

'Eh? What?'

'Hardly a blind word since I picked you up. That's not natural, see?'

'I'm — er — I'm not very talkative. That's all.'

'Poor company.'

'I'm — I'm sorry.'

'You seem frightened of something, mate. Scared.'

'No! It's not that. I'm just . . .'

'I don't want any stumers, that's all. If you *are* . . .'

'No, I'm not. If you'll — if you'll excuse me, I — er — I'd like to visit the toilet.'

Then he'd hurried out into the night, screwed up his courage and begged another lift. To where? To *anywhere*, away from a man asking too many of the wrong questions.

Holmes was dumb. Holmes hadn't the simple gumption to realise that the very act of running away had confirmed suspicions; that squad-car coppers visit all-night transport cafes during their tours of duty; that the long-distance boys liaise with the law when they think things are seriously wrong and that the tight world of H.G.V. drivers holds few secrets concerning probable destinations.

Nevertheless, Holmes was in Birmingham, Holmes had less than two pounds in his pockets and Holmes was scared. Hell's teeth, he'd never seen such a maze of dual carriageways, cross-overs and cross-unders. They built cars in these parts. By the weight of traffic few of the cars they built ever *left* these parts.

He found a side street and in the side street he found a cafe. His life it would seem was a dash from one cheap hash joint to another. From one slash-house to another. He found the toilet, relieved his bursting bladder, then edged his way to the counter and ordered tea. It went in up top, it came out down bottom. Christ, he was a bag filled with liquid. A hole at the top and a hole at the bottom, and damn-all in between.

He sipped tea and wondered what had happened to Innes. What had happened to Solly. What was going to happen to *him*.

He craved for a smoke, but was out of cigarettes and couldn't find the nerve to approach the counter again to buy a packet.

They'd wrung Quince dry. They'd squeezed every fact, near-fact, rumour and rumour of rumour from his miserable, deformed little body. They'd left him as flat and deflated as an unused loofah on the shelves of a chemist's shop. And now they were back at the Murder Room, reporting the direction of their enquiries to the man in charge.

To Adamson it seemed a strangely pointless exercise. Flensing gave the impression of being only mildly interested. Almost indifferent.

'You believe him?' he murmured.

'I believe he's told us all he knows and all he thinks he knows,' said Hoyle.

'That Manford's our man?'

'That it's a possibility,' said Hoyle carefully.

'Could he?' Flensing asked the question of Adamson.

Adamson said, 'He's cell-happy. That's what Quince thinks.'

'I wasn't asking Quince.'

'I think *anybody* could commit murder,' said Adamson bluntly.

'Not a philosophical discussion. Manford?'

'He has a list. A long list. He was a violent man.'

'Was?'

'I think he's turned straight.'

'Does such an animal exist?' drawled Flensing.

'Sir, with respect . . .'

'Which means you're going to be very *dis*respectful.'

'. . . if it doesn't we're all wasting our bloody time.'

In a soft voice, but without contempt, Flensing said, 'We have a dreamer in our ranks, chief inspector.' Then, without change of tone, to Hoyle, 'Elsie Manford.'

'She has to be found,' sighed Hoyle. 'Dead or alive.'

'If dead, murder number two.'

'It would seem so.'

Flensing moved his head and stared past Hoyle and Adamson. He gave the impression of gazing at a sky-line beyond that of normal sight; at a point on a far distant horizon seen only by himself. Stone-faced and with world-weary eyes. When he spoke, the gentle laconic quality was missing; the words were sardonic, but the tone was flat and without life.

'Not what any of us expected, gentlemen. Not what we *ever* expect. The neat clues of the detective novel. The footprint in the soil of the flower bed. The conveniently detatched button from the murderer's coat. Speaking personally, I've never come across a so-called "locked-room mystery". I wish a search for the truth was as easy as that. As uncomplicated. Instead, we chase shadows and encounter other shadows. Our lords and masters — the rate-payers and tax-payers — insist that we chase *those* shadows, too. A shadowy world, gentlemen. But which shadows are important, and which should we ignore?' He paused, still gazing with unfocussed eyes beyond the walls of the room, then continued, 'They're all the same in death. Gatling, Daniels, the Manford girl . . . if, indeed, she is dead. They feel nothing. All future anguish, all future worries, they're all cancelled out. The killer can have done a great favour, but that side of things must never be emphasised. Never so much as mentioned. The ultimate crime . . . but I can think of worse things.'

The eyes came back into focus, and he said, 'What's his name? Jakeman?'

'John Jakeman, sir,' said Adamson. '"Jumbo" to his friends.'

'We don't want him to disappear.'

Hoyle said, 'I'll arrange for round-the-clock surveillance.'

'As soon as possible, please. Before you push this line any further. Before somebody whispers words of warning into his ear.'

'Yes, sir.'

'And the Manford woman? The mother?'

'Her next, I thought.'

'Here.' Flensing breathed a little deeply. It might have been a repressed sigh but, if it was, no accompanying expression touched either the face or the eyes. 'On our own ground and before her husband gets home from work. I'd like to sit in on the interview, chief inspector.'

'Of course.'

'A policewoman to pick her up. Tell her nothing. Allow her own conscience — assuming she has one — to do the groundwork for us. And surveillance on her husband too, I think. Unobtrusive, of course. Until things are established one way or the other.'

'Yes, sir.' Hoyle cleared his throat, then said, 'Chief Inspector

King, sir.'

'When do you expect him to relieve you?'

'I — er . . .' Hoyle looked surprised.

'Two men with initiative,' said Flensing. 'Each in his own way responsible for the hour-by-hour conduct of the enquiry. They'd be fools if they didn't share the load.'

'Yes, sir,' said Hoyle with a smile. 'Two o'clock, sir.'

'I think *you'd* better continue this particular red herring.'

'Yes, sir.'

'Have lunch. See Mr King. Arrange things with him as you see fit.'

'Yes, sir. We'll work something out.'

'And you, Constable Adamson. Stay with it . . . red herring or not. All the way. It's your beat. That gives you the edge on all of us.'

Spud Murphy. The presumption was that he'd once had a first name. That at some time in the mists of the past he'd had parents and had, by the nature of things, been christened. *He* didn't know. Nobody knew. He was Spud Murphy . . . period.

He was "pixilated". That was a polite way of putting it. In blunter language, he was a raving lunatic. His home was a broken down caravan in a car-wrecker's yard; a single, fibre-glass box without light, without water, without sanitation. For illumination he used candles. For heat he used a near-lethal paraffin stove.

But a most happy man. A most friendly man.

His constant companion was a cracked and warped violin. An abortive thing; the very afterbirth of a musical instrument. Yet Yehudi Menuhin could not have loved a fiddle more. He carried it around in a cheap cardboard suitcase. He drew the almost hairless bow across the badly tuned strings and, in a sheltered corner of the pedestrian precinct, scraped out his own version of *If You Were The Only Girl In The World*. Over and over again, because that was the only tune he knew; the only tune his befuddled brain could hold. With coins dropped into the open suitcase he bought candles, paraffin, cheap tea, the occasional luxury of fresh milk, but for the rest he begged stale bread, bruised fruit, rotting vegetables and meat on the "off".

A strangely contented man, in that life had taught him to expect nothing. A man unworried and unaffected, by national and

95

international events. What matter if world statesmen played brinksmanship roulette with the rest of mankind? Spud Murphy had shelter, food and warmth; enough to keep his skinny body ticking over. What other concerns should Spud Murphy torment his mind with?

He squatted on his haunches, held the fiddle to his ear, plucked a string and fiddled around with the wrong peg.

'A nice feller,' he said cheerfully. 'A very nice feller. Stops to chat every time we meet, he does.'

'He won't chat any . . .'

'Not many fellers do that, y'know. Too busy they are. Too busy with their own business. Not Fred Kelly, though. Fred Kelly always stops for a chat.'

'He won't . . .'

'What did you say your name was, mister?'

'Ballester. Detective Sergeant Ballester.'

'I'll tell him next time I see him. I'll tell him you were asking after him.'

'You won't . . .' Ballester closed his mouth, changed mental gear and tried to go along the same track as Murphy. 'Had he — er — *has* he any enemies?'

'Who?' Murphy continued to pluck the violin string.

'Kelly. Your friend, Fred Kelly.'

'Enemies?'

'Aye.'

'Now, Mr Bannister . . .'

'Ballester.'

'. . . why should a lovely man like Fred Kelly have enemies? What a question to ask. A man who stops to have a quiet chat every time he sees me. I can't think where you get the idea from that a man like that might have enemies.'

'Gatling,' said Ballester.

'Who?'

'Sammy Gatling. Mean anything?'

'Somebody I know, is it?'

'That's what I'm asking.'

'Well now, Mr Cannister . . .'

'Ballester . . .'

'. . . with a man like me, I know so many people, y'see. Men and women. And kids. I'm very popular with the kids, y'see.

They like the way I play. They like music, kids do. They all like music. I've known . . .'

'Gatling,' interrupted Ballester.

'Who?'

'Sammy Gatling.' Desperation was creeping into Ballester's tone. 'Let's stay with Sammy Gatling?'

'Who's Sammy Gatling?'

'Christ Almighty! Stop twanging that bloody string and *listen*.'

Spud Murphy obligingly lowered the violin. It left him one hand free, therefore he began to pick his nose.

'Sammy Gatling,' choked Ballester.

'Who's Sam . . .'

'All right! Fred Kelly.'

'A nice man. A lovely man. He always stops to . . .'

'*Who didn't like him*?' bawled Ballester.

'Who?'

'Fred Kelly.'

With a forefinger well up his left nostril Spud Murphy eyed Ballester with a worried frown as he said, 'Mr Bassiter . . .'

'*Ballester*.'

'. . . that's not a nice thing to say.'

'What?'

'Fred won't like it when I tell him.'

'How in hell can Fred . . .'

'I wouldn't like to think anybody called Guzzling didn't like *me*, that I tell you.'

'Guzzling?'

'You just said somebody called Sammy Guzzling doesn't like . . .'

'*Gatling*!'

'All right. I don't know the man. Don't want to know him. If he doesn't like Fred, he doesn't like me. So, I don't like him. Why come here and spread trouble, that's what I'd like to know. What's it to you whether somebody likes me or doesn't like me? I get along.'

Not a patient man, nevertheless Ballester was a sticker. Somewhere under this mad nerk's hairline there might be information, added to which he (Ballester) was loth to admit that *he* might be an equally mad nerk in pursuing this line of enquiry. He hung on with his fingernails for almost thirty minutes. He damn near took that bloody violin and wrapped it around Spud Murphy's grubby little neck. Then, reluctantly, he capitulated.

'Forget it,' he croaked. 'Forget you ever saw me.'

'And why should I do that? You come here, you . . .'

'As a personal favour. It's all been a dream.'

He staggered from the caravan, threaded a slightly unsteady way through the snow-covered piles of motor-car innards and sought some degree of sanity in the nearest boozer. Unfortunately, that boozer was The Bunch Of Grapes. An establishment where, for the moment, policemen did not top the popularity poll.

To peer into another man's life. To open drawers and cupboards, uptip mattresses and empty pockets, clear every shelf and every box of its contents. Coppers do these things when necessary, but rarely enjoy doing them. It smacks too much of voyeurism; of peeking through chinks in curtains.

Lowe and Ellis obeyed orders with the objectivity of long practice. The table in the main downstairs room of the house in Chamber's Court became filled with the trifles of an ended life. Valueless things which were, at the same time, priceless. Playing cards; three well-thumbed packs, one with the four of spades torn across its surface and repaired with yellowing Sellotape. A collection of old ballpoint pens; cheap and of various colours, most of them empty and useless. Tattered paperbacks; curled pages and soiled covers, more than half of them cheap Westerns written by unknown authors. An unpaid gas bill. A postcard-sized photograph of a neatly-dressed, well-scrubbed boy wearing a skull-cap on the back of his head; the photograph carefully stored and kept clean inside a folded paper bag.

'Bar mitzvah,' grunted Lowe.

Ellis said, 'That means orthodox.'

'They lapse, like everybody else.'

Nevertheless, they placed the photograph to one side. A bar mitzvah meant a synagogue, and a synagogue meant a Rabbi . . . and that *might* give a lead to a next-of-kin.

A few old magazines, some out-of-date newspapers, but no letters, no postcards, no telephone numbers, not even a jotted-down address.

'Unloved, unwanted,' observed Ellis grimly.

'He didn't even *exist*.' Lowe's tone was sadder than that of Ellis. 'Not even a birth certificate.'

There are some very comfortable and highly respectable hotels and guest houses within easy walking distance of King's Cross Station. Not quite in the Hotel Intercontinental class, of course, but hell you don't expect Napoleonic brandy at mild-and-bitter prices. But they are not *all* respectable and, unfortunately, Innes was a bad picker. And the guy whose work-card read "Hall Porter" was in the world class when it came to spotting a juicy lift.

'That bag.' He was sharing secrets with his colleague, the so-called "Head Waiter". He tapped the side of a nostril knowingly. 'That zip bag. Something, mate. *Something*.'

His colleague expressed interested surprise, and the hall porter confided, 'Knackered, mate. Completely knackered, when he arrived. Out on his bleedin' feet. But would he let me carry that bag to his room? No, mate. Wouldn't let me touch it. Fourth floor, but he wouldn't let me near the thing. Gripping it, see? All the way up the stairs. And asking. "Is there a lock on the door?" Three times, he asked. Something, mate. *Something*.'

His colleague agreed there was "something".

The hall porter amplified, 'Down from up North.' (He pronounced it "Darn from hip Norf".) 'Tell from his talk. A right bleedin' hick. Shouldn't be allowed out.' He glanced at the wall clock. 'Should be fast asleep by now. Out to the wide. I think we should take the master key and investigate.'

Little more than ten minutes later they were in the bedroom and, having checked upon the sleeping Innes, were ready to unzip the holdall and eye the goodies.

Then things happened quite suddenly. A car, four floors down, in the street backfired. It was a hell of a backfire, and it nudged Innes from his sleep enough for him to become aware that he was not alone. He grunted, then yelled, then grabbed for the pillow. The two would-be-thieves dived for the door as Innes brought the Colt .32 from under the pillow, pointed it and, almost as a reflex action, squeezed the trigger. Then the hall porter yelled as the slug ploughed a neat furrow across the right cheek of his backside.

After which, it only took time.

Four storeys up is no place from which to plan a sudden escape route. Innes was still in the bedroom, wondering what the hell to do next, when the two officers from D Division arrived. Politely, but firmly, one of the officers called from the passage and explained that, unless Innes threw the firearm out of the door, then followed it with his hands clasped firmly at the back of his neck, that officer would come into the bedroom, take the gun, ram it down Innes's throat and proceed to shoot his balls off the hard way.

Innes believed him. The London cops were capable of *anything*.

And that was Innes taken care of.

FOUR

Chief Superintendent Rupert Johnstone felt out of things. Which wasn't good enough. He was the guy with the crowns and pips; the guy with the omelet around the peak of his cap. What was more, North End was *his* division. When all the hoo-ha of this ridiculous enquiry had quietened down — when Flensing had returned to his own office at Lessford Regional Headquarters to do the job for which he was paid — he (Johnstone) would have the unenviable task of "putting things right". All that was ahead, of course, and something not to be anticipated with any degree of pleasure and yet, despite this, he felt he was being left out of things.

He sailed into the Murder Room prepared to assert his undoubted authority, saw the sergeant clerk bent over a sheaf of papers at the main desk, and demanded, 'Where's Chief Inspector King?'

'Sir?' The sergeant clerk looked up then stood up.

'Inspector King,' repeated Johnstone. 'He's supposed to be in charge, here. Where is he?'

'Er — on at two, sir.' The sergeant clerk saw no reason to be other than honest; to pass on what he'd been told. Chief superintendents were supposed to know what was going on, and that Johnstone obviously *didn't* was (presumably) due to some minor breakdown in communication. He glanced at his watch, and added, 'Within the next twenty minutes, or so.'

'Indeed?' Johnstone compressed his lips. 'On at two?'

'Yes, sir.'

'Indeed?' repeated Johnstone. 'And where is Chief Superintendent Flensing?'

'In Number One Interview Room, sir. He's with . . .'

'I'm not interested in who he's *with*,' snapped Johnstone petulantly. 'Just that he's *there*. That somebody with rank knows what is and what isn't going on.'

Johnstone marched, stiff-backed from the Murder Room.

'Nice,' observed a constable clerk gently and winked at the

sergeant.

'And naughty,' added the sergeant clerk.

'Sooner him than me.'

Number One Interview Room had been modernised. Civilisation, of a sort, had even crept into police interview rooms. The table was Formica-surfaced. The floor was vinyl tiled. The chairs were of tubular steel and canvas with arm-rests. Even the cheap tin ash-tray (filched from some pub counter) had been replaced by one of heavy glass and large enough to take all the cigarette ends likely to be squashed out even during a prolonged interview. The window was of "picture" size, but paned with pebbled glass. The strip-lighting was still there, but the walls were of ivory-coloured gloss paint, applied by a craftsman, and there was even a wall-mounted telephone. All mod cons one might say and far less intimidating than the old-fashioned "sweat box" type in which once-upon-a-time suspects had been asked awkward questions. Indeed, to some of the visitors Number One Interview Room was a great improvement, in furnishings and cleanliness, to any rooms in their own homes.

And yet, despite these changes, still an interview room. Still a place of shame-faced truth teased from men (and sometimes women) who entered with self-assurance, but left with the fear of their confessions haunting their expressions. "Our own ground" Flensing had called it, and that's what the interview room (any interview room) was; the furnishings and decoration counted for nothing when you were *there* — officially or unofficially, arrested or merely "asked" — you were undoubtably in police custody. You were surrounded by coppers and all the trappings of police authority.

As Johnstone burst into the room without knocking the woman was settling herself in the chair by the table. Opposite her across the table sat Hoyle. At one end of the table in a third chair Adamson had placed a clipboard holding sheets of foolscap on the surface of the table and was fishing around in his breast pocket feeling for a ballpoint. Flensing was relaxed in a chair in one corner of the room, behind and to one side of the woman, and well out of her line of vision.

'Ah, Flensing,' barked Johnson, 'I'd like a word . . .'

'Constable Adamson.' Flensing uncurled himself from his chair as he interrupted Johnstone's irate outburst. 'Rustle up Mrs Manford a cup of tea. Four cups of tea in fact. And some biscuits, if the petty cash can stand the strain.'

'Yes, sir.' Adamson placed the ballpoint carefully alongside the clipboard, having dragged his gaze from the flushed face and popping eyes of his divisional chief superintendent.

As Adamson pushed back his chair, Flensing's fingers tightened around Johnstone's elbow, and the detective chief superintendent said, 'A word with you, please, Mr Johnstone. In the privacy of your office, if you don't mind.'

'I don't see what . . .'

'But *I* do.' Flensing's lips moved into a rare smile. 'Certain confidential information I think you should know.'

'Oh! In that case . . .'

Flensing turned the uniformed chief superintendent towards the door and murmured, *'Confidential,* Mr Johnstone. For your ears only.'

'Ah!'

They walked along corridors, not quite side by side, not quite Indian-file fashion, but Johnstone leading the way. They reached a door marked "Divisional Officer" and Johnstone opened the door and stood aside to let Flensing pass. Neither of them spoke until Johnstone had closed the door.

'Now, what was it . . .' began Johnstone.

'Who the hell told you you were a policeman?' asked Flensing gently. He hitched a buttock onto the surface of Johnstone's desk and amplified, 'Which purblind idiot suggested you were a fit and capable man to strut around dressed like a senior police officer?'

'Look! I don't know what . . .'

'Shut up!' The volume was no greater, but the naked contempt made it as vicious and as silencing as a whip lash. Flensing's half-closed eyes surveyed Johnstone in silence for a moment, much like an entomologist might examine a new species of particularly disgusting bug, then he said, 'That was an interview room, Johnstone. An interview room . . . in use.'

'I'm aware of that.' Johnstone moved towards his chair behind the desk. 'I'm also aware . . .'

'Don't sit down, Johnstone.' Flensing held out his arm as a barrier. 'Don't take up a position in the seat of the Almighty. This time it's not some pipsqueak, green recruit you're out to impress. I match you rank for rank and, in a major crime enquiry, I *out*-rank you. That being the case, understand me. Understand me well. *I'm* doing the ballocking this time.'

'How dare you? How dare you . . .'

'Oh, I dare. You'd be surprised. I dare fizz you, if necessary. And *will*, unless you stop puffing and spluttering and throwing weight around you don't possess.'

The shock silenced Johnstone; the shock that *anybody* could quietly, almost casually, talk to him and threaten him in this manner. Nevertheless, there was about Flensing that air of off-handed certainty which precluded any hint of bluff.

Flensing said, 'At recruit training depots, they teach men — men not yet allowed loose on the streets — that an interview room, when in use, is inviolate. It must not be entered except in dire emergency . . . and then only after knocking and waiting to be invited to enter. An *interview* room, Johnstone. A room where criminals and suspected criminals are *interviewed*. Where, after great patience, and no little cunning, a point of balance is sometimes reached. A very delicate balance. Will he, won't he? Will she, won't she? The difference between a detected crime and an undetected crime. The difference between success and a monumental waste of time and money. Not, therefore, a place to rush into as if diving through the swing-doors of some four-ale bar hoping to catch the pumps before closing time.'

Johnstone gasped, 'I — I didn't . . .'

'You *did*. The only thing missing was a military band.'

'I mean . . . I didn't *mean* to . . .'

'Johnstone, I wouldn't take that excuse from a man off a beat, much less from a man wearing *that* regalia.'

Johnstone had the wit to see personal catastrophe rushing towards him at a rare rate of knots. He back-pedalled as hard as possible.

'Look, I'm very sorry, Ralph. Dammit, you don't think . . .'

'No!' The eyes glittered beneath those drooping lids.

'What?' Johnstone moved his hands in tiny gestures of helplessness. 'I mean what am I supposed to . . .'

'Not the first name, Johnstone. I have few friends — very few — and they are allowed. You? *Never.*'

'Look, I didn't mean to sound . . .'

'What's it about?' asked Flensing in a tired voice.

'Eh?'

'The all-singing-all-dancing entry to the interview room. You wanted to see *me*. What about?'

'Oh! Er . . .' Johnstone grabbed for excuses. 'Just that — y'know — Hoyle and King. That they're pulling their weight.'

'They are,' said Flensing in a flat tone.

'Good. In that case . . .'

'Keep clear of this enquiry, Johnstone,' said Flensing. 'Well clear.'

'Of course. Look, if I've given the impression . . .'

'Keep clear of the Murder Room.'

'If — if that's what you . . .'

'That's what I want.'

'In that case, I'll . . .'

'Keep clear of every officer engaged on the enquiry.'

'I say — look — that's going a bit . . .'

'All of them.'

'Well — all right — if that's what . . .'

'Above all else, keep clear of *me*. Otherwise I will personally, expertly and very happily emasculate you.'

By early afternoon the snow had eased off; occasional flurries not, as before, periods of sustained and heavy fall. A slight thaw had set in and even the sky looked less solid grey than it had for days.

Lowe stared out of the grimy window of the house in Chamber's Court, and said, 'Always the same.'

'What's that?' asked Ellis.

'Snow for Christmas. There never is. Before and after, but never on the day. Ever noticed that?'

'Now you mention it,' murmured Ellis.

They were in a house — in a room — where, to their certain knowledge, a man had taken his own life within the last twenty-four hours. They were coppers, but they were also human beings. There was a "feel" about the place. The primaeval fear of the unknown touched them. The veneer of civilisation — the down-to-earth authority of the uniform — was not enough to keep all that fear at bay.

Ellis eyed the pile of junk on the table and said 'Not much.'

'Nothing.' Lowe turned from the window. 'No identification. No bank book, no driving licence, no rate bill. Nothing. The poor sod didn't even exist.'

'The Bar mitzvah photograph?'

'Is it *him*?' countered Lowe.

'If not . . .' Ellis moved his shoulders.

Lowe said, 'Assuming it *is*. A photograph taken by who knows who, who knows where. Something he kept. Proof that he once *was*.'

'As you say. The poor sod.'

Flensing was back in the chair he'd vacated when Johnstone had burst into Number One Interview Room. He was relaxed, with his legs crossed, his bunched hands thrust deep into the pockets of his jacket and his eyes almost closed. He gave the impression of settling down for a quiet cat-nap.

The woman, Edwina Manford, had retrieved some of her composure. When Johnstone had arrived she'd been frightened. She'd been made to *feel* frightened. The call at her home by the woman police sergeant; the request to come to the police station; the silent, almost solemn ride in the squad car. She'd asked questions — obvious questions — but had received no real answer.

'What do they want to see me for?'

'They'll tell you when we get there.'

'Who? Who's "they"?'

'Detective Chief Inspector Hoyle.'

'What's he want to see *me* about?'

'He'll tell you.'

'I've done nowt wrong.'

'Haven't you?'

'Well, *have* I?'

'You know best.'

'All right. What *have* I done wrong?'

'According to you, nothing.'

'That's a daft answer.'

'It'll have to do, until Chief Inspector Hoyle sees you.'

That sort of thing. Therefore, by the time she'd been plonked down in the interview room, she was ripe for the gathering. Ready to talk, fifty-to-the-dozen if necessary, just to get somebody to answer a few simple qustions.

But by the time Flensing had returned from Johnstone's office

— by the time tea and biscuits had been delivered — some of the composure had returned. It showed, too. In the near-arrogant way in which she'd lighted a cigarette, then lazily dropped the spent match into the ash-tray. Her steady hold of the cup and saucer as she sipped tea. The eye-to-eye reply to the basic questions — full name, address, age and occupation — as Adamson filled in the heading on the first foolscap sheet.

And now she waited, hard-eyed and suspicious as Hoyle steepled his fingers and said, 'The murder of Samuel Gatling, Mrs Manford.'

'I can read.'

'Of course.' Hoyle smiled gently. 'It's held headlines in the locals. Quite a mention in some of the nationals.'

'I know what I've read. That's all I know.'

'You knew *him*,' contradicted Hoyle.

'What's that mean?'

'As a person. You knew him.'

'Why not? Everybody knew him.'

'And?'

'*I* didn't kill him.'

'Get that down, constable.' Hoyle turned to Adamson. 'When asked whether she knew Gatling, the interviewee replied "I didn't kill him".'

Manford protested, 'Look, that's not what . . .'

'What you said, surely?'

'Not that *way*. It makes it sound as if . . .'

'As if you *might* have killed him?'

'Just as it stands, it sounds as if . . .'

'You might *know* who killed him.'

'Look, mister, you're putting words into my mouth.'

'No.' Hoyle shook his head. 'Your own words, with possible meanings.'

The cigarette she was smoking travelled to her lips and back. A quick, nervous journey. The interview room was spinning its subtle magic. That and a man who knew how to ask questions — how to phrase them — and never believe the answers.

Hoyle asked, 'How well did you know Sammy Gatling?'

'Not . . .' She moistened her lips. 'Not all that well.'

'You work at The Bunch of Grapes.'

'Yeah. I serve . . .'

'Behind the bar.'

'Yeah.'

'Every day.'

'Yeah. Every evening.'

'Gatling's pub?'

'Yeah. Well — one of a few . . .'

'His *favourite* pub?'

'Yeah. You could say that.'

'Every evening.'

'What?'

'He visited the pub every evening?'

'Yeah . . . I suppose.'

'He knew you by your first name.'

'They all do. That doesn't mean . . .'

'You knew *him* by *his* first name.'

'Look, mister, where have you been living all you life. It's a pub. I work behind the bar. Gatling was a regular customer. In every night. *Sure* we knew each other. A quiet night . . . we'd talk. Tell each other things, just to pass the time. That's not . . .'

'That's not knowing somebody "not all that well",' said Hoyle, gently.

The trick. To give the impression of accepting an answer. To continue the interview, and steer the conversation to a point where that original answer doesn't make sense. To force a contradiction, point out that contradiction, then change the subject.

Hoyle said, 'Let's talk about Jumbo Jakeman.'

'Attempted murder.' The D Division inspector grinned down at the quaking Innes. 'Attempted murder, more than two hundred thousand smackers and a shooter he hasn't a certificate for. Who's a naughty boy, then?'

'You can't call it attempted murder,' pleaded Innes. 'It only . . .'

'You were trying to shoot him up the arse,' said the sergeant, cheerfully. 'Not a nice way to kill a man.'

Innes stared in turn at his two tormentors. Big men. Happy men. If he didn't co-operate they'd break his arms and legs and continue to smile. Innes had heard stories about the Big City, *and* about the fuzz who policed the Big City.

'Do you cough now?' asked the inspector with a smile. 'Or do you cough later?'

'Christ!' breathed Innes. 'Attempted murder.'

'It rolls off the tongue,' agreed the inspector.

'Tell us what happened, Innes,' coaxed the sergeant. 'In simple, cat-sat-on-the-mat language. We're slow on the uptake down here. We need to be *told*. Every little detail. Otherwise, we don't latch on. And if we don't latch on . . .'

'Don't tell him, sergeant,' interrupted the inspector with smile. 'Let it come as a surprise.'

'I'll — I'll talk,' whispered Innes. 'I'll cough. What is it you want to know?'

'We're open to suggestions,' said the inspector.

'Any reasonable offer,' added the sergeant.

Hoyle was building up a rapport with Edwina Manford. Slowly. To ease trust from her. To make her forget where she was, and who and what *he* was.

'Jakeman was Gatling's pal.'

'Oh, sure. Thick as thieves, as the saying goes.'

'They probably *were* thieves,' smiled Hoyle.

'I wouldn't die of shock.'

The cigarette rose to the over-painted lips. She inhaled, then allowed the smoke to trickle down her nostrils.

'Could he have killed Gatling?' asked Hoyle gently.

'Who? Jakeman?'

Hoyle nodded and watched the woman's face.

'He *could* have,' she said slowly. 'But I don't think he *would* have.'

'Too friendly?'

'I reckon.'

'Never any squabbles? Never any tiffs?'

'Not that I know of.'

'Jakeman and Gatling,' mused Hoyle. 'Quite a combination from what I hear. Anything.'

'Eh?'

'Anything,' repeated Hoyle. 'From a suite of furniture to a bottle of cough medicine. All from the backs of lorries. That's what I'm told.'

'About right,' she admitted.

Adamson recorded the conversation on foolscap. He used

111

question and answer form; starting a new line each time the talk switched from Hoyle to the woman, or from the woman back to Hoyle. He was a moderately fast writer and, whenever the words came faster that his ballpoint could record them, he fell back on his own form of shorthand.

One part of his mind concentrated upon writing down the words spoken, but another part of his mind caught and admired the gist and direction of the interview. First Gatling. Now Jakeman. Dummy bullets to give her a false sense of safety until the live rounds — questions about her daughter and her husband — were lined up on an unprotected target.

'How did you get on with Jakeman?' asked Hoyle.

'Who? Me?'

'About on a par with Gatling?'

'Look, I don't see what you've brought me here for. I can't tell you . . .'

'To get a picture,' interrupted Hoyle soothingly. 'Gatling. Somebody killed Gatling. We're out to name that person. That means we need background to point us in the general direction. We can't just swan around, staking everything on blind hope and good fortune.'

'I still don't see what I . . .'

'The boozer. The Bunch of Grapes. We've already talked to Quince. Seen Mrs Quince. You're next on the list. That's all it . . .'

'What did *they* say?' she cut in, and her voice was a little too loud, a little too anxious.

'Oh, no.' Hoyle shook his head slowly. He smiled as he continued, 'We don't work that way, Mrs Manford. Quince and his wife tell us things. *They* know what they've told us. *We* know what they've told us. But that's as far as it goes. Nobody else.'

'I wouldn't trust Quince,' she muttered savagely.

'Of course not. Nobody, until we know.' He paused then, as if on an impulse, said, 'Right. Let's talk about Quince.'

It was all Reg Innes's fault, of course. Who else? Smacking a man in the chops like that. And for what? For making a bad call. That important. That earth-shattering. Letting fly and sending poor old Sammy backwards, and making him catch his noggin on the stove. Then not telling anybody. Not *telling* anybody. The cops . . . they should have been told. An accident. Nothing *wrong*. Not murder. For Christ's sake, not *murder*! Tell the cops then. When it had happened. All this talk about murder wouldn't have built up.

Then letting Innes take over. Getting rid of a stiff the Innes way. Holy cow! The bread van, the sheet, some other poor bugger's grave. Nobody was going to believe *that*.

Don't kid yourself, Holmes old son. It's murder. It wasn't at first, but by this time it will be. The cops'll see to that. Pigs galore and the pantomime season in full swing. They daren't let it *not* be murder.

He saw the sign which read "B.R. Station" and followed the line of its pointing arm. A main line railway station. Somewhere where people don't know each other. A whole crowd of strangers, all coming from or going to. A place to get lost. *Really* lost. Maybe a kiosk where he could buy fags. Maybe a newspaper and see what was happening.

He quickened his step slightly . . .

Edwina Manford said, 'He was safer at the other side of the bar. At our side, he couldn't keep his hands to himself.'

'As bad as that?' murmured Hoyle politely.

'Better now, of course. He behaves himself these days.'

'Why is that?'

'His wife tumbled. They must have had a hell of a row after closing time. They wouldn't talk to each other for more than a week.'

'Not quite the way he puts it,' said Hoyle.

'No — well — he wouldn't, would he?'

'His wife wasn't there,' teased Hoyle.

'I don't see what . . .'

'There was no reason for him not telling the truth.'

'About what?'

'You two. You and him.'

'What's he been saying?' Her eyes narrowed and gleamed. 'What's the lying hound been saying?'

'Extra marital jinks.'

'The lousy, lying . . .'

'. . . and something about an abortifacient.'

'A what?'

'An abortifacient for your daughter. About two years ago.'

113

It stopped her dead. It closed her mouth, and the gleam in her eyes was no longer a reflection of outrage.

'To bring about a miscarriage,' said Hoyle softly. 'An approach he made on your behalf. To Gatling and Jakeman.'

'Oh, God,' she breathed, 'is Elsie going to be dragged into it?'

'Can Elsie be left out of it?' countered Hoyle.

'You — you wanted to see me about Gatling's murder. That's what you said when I arrived. Just a few questions about . . .'

'About Gatling.'

'Yeah, but not about . . .'

'Gatling,' repeated Hoyle. 'Gatling and your daughter. Do I have to spell it out before you believe we know?'

An opened packet of cigarettes was on the table. She reached across and with a near-snatching motion picked up the packet. She fumbled for a cigarette, spilled three onto the table, then closed her lips around one of them. Hoyle held out a lighter, and she had to hold the cigarette between thumb and forefinger in order to keep it steady enough to rest in the flame.

Hoyle allowed her time for two deep inhalations of cigarette smoke, then he said, 'Your husband was inside at the time. Right?'

'Yeah.' She nodded jerkily.

'Your daughter was pregnant?'

'Yeah.'

'Gatling was the father?'

'Yeah.'

'That's it then.' Hoyle leaned back in his chair. 'Take it from there, and let's see if your story dovetails into what we already know.'

The press liaison bloke was chairing his afternoon flannel session. He was uniform chief inspector, chubby faced and shiny. As smooth as the non-answers he fed to media people. In the rough and tumble of street policing he'd have been cat's meat within the first twenty-four hours, but this wasn't street policing. This was merely saying sweet nothings to pencil-wielding yucks who figured they were going to perform a Bernstein/Woodward re-run.

Yes, certain people were "helping in the enquiries".

No, he was in no position, as yet, to give names.

Yes, certain motives were "under consideration".

~~No, he was in no position, as yet, to give names.~~
~~Yes, certain motives were "under consideration".~~

The usual crap. *He* knew it, *they* knew it, but what the hell? They'd have asked around. They'd know the sort of creep Gatling had been. It wasn't a tear-jerker. Without the sheet, without the take-over of an opened grave, it wouldn't have deserved a mention in the nationals. But a murder with a kinky angle made good breakfast time reading.

One of the local reporters said, 'Edwina Manford. Is *she* under suspicion?'

The press liaison bloke blocked that one by saying, 'Nobody's yet under suspicion.'

'But she's inside. In one of the interview rooms.'

'Is she?' countered the press liaison bloke blandly.

A man from one of the nationals said, 'You mean you don't *know*?'

'Certainly I know.' The press liaison bloke lost some of his cool. He snapped, 'I've already said. She's helping with the enquiries.'

'Not her old man?' the local reporter pushed.

'Who?'

'Bill Manford. William Manford. Not *him*?'

'In — er — in due course.' Then, the press liaison bloke realised he'd said a little too much, and added, 'Perhaps.'

The press liaison bloke scurried back into his office, but the newspaper hounds hung around and asked questions of the local reporter and, because he had visions of Fleet Street and a regular by-line, the local reporter happily amplified upon his theme of William and Edwina Manford. Who they were, where they lived and what they'd each done to earn their respective reputations.

She told the story in tiny hurried sentences, with gaps of silence between. Like crossing a torrent via stepping-stones; ensuring steady balance before moving to the next slab. Nor was it told chronologically. The excuses often preceded the incidents. 'It's not easy when your husband's inside.'

Nobody interrupted her. Nobody prompted her. It was her story, told in her own way. 'She was a little madam. *I* couldn't handle her.' And, always, the fault wasn't hers. 'Dammit, a man like Gatling. He should have had more sense. More decency. She

115

was little more than a child.' And gradually the gaps lengthened, the sentences became shorter, until she ended, 'And that's it.'

'Not by a country mile.' Flensing eased himself from his chair, glanced at Hoyle and said, 'D'you mind?'

'Not at all.'

Hoyle stood up and he and Flensing exchanged chairs. The detective chief superintendent gazed across the table, as if memorising the woman's face for future reference. The silence reached upwards towards screaming point before he spoke.

'A personal assessment of Gatling,' he murmured. '*Your* assessment. He's dead. He can't sue you.'

'A bloody animal,' she breathed.

'Responsible for your daughter being — what is it? — "with child"?'

'Yeah.'

'But other than that?'

'Dopey. Thick. He couldn't . . .'

'You trusted him with your daughter's life.'

'Yeah — well — how was I to know . . .'

'Back-street abortions,' he said, softly. 'Nasty. Deadly. You didn't mind *that*.'

'Yeah — well — Bill was inside and . . .'

'And you were taking tumbles in the hay.'

'Yeah,' she breathed.

'How much did it cost?' he asked.

'Eh?'

'Madam,' said Flensing, 'we're living in the real world. Money buys things. The only give-away line is misery. How much did the abortion cost?'

'A hundred.' She paused then added, 'To Jakeman for the stuff.'

'Nothing to Gatling?'

'It was Gatling's *fault*.'

'Partly,' agreed Flensing dryly. 'And the last time you saw your daughter she was leaving the house with Gatling?'

'To meet Jakeman.'

'Who had the elixir of happiness?'

'Eh?'

'"The stuff", as you call it.'

116

'Oh! Yeah.'

'You didn't go with them?'

'Eh?' She looked surprised. 'God, no.'

'Why not?'

'Something like that. I wanted no part.'

'And who says maternal concern is on the down slope?'

'Eh?'

'What next?'

'Gatling came back. Said things had gone wrong.'

'Wrong?'

'I dunno. I didn't ask.'

'Meaning your daughter was dead?'

'What else?'

'You pressed him on the point?'

'Yeah. Sure.'

'That your daughter was dead?'

'Yeah, I pressed him. She was my kid wasn't she?'

'That must have given her more than a few moments of high delight.'

'Look, I had worries of my own. If the silly little cow . . .'

'The body?' interrupted Flensing.

'Eh?'

'Your daughter. There was a body. What happened to it?'

'I — I didn't ask.'

'Sweet God Almighty!'

'I had my own troubles. If — if Bill found out about me . . . well, you know what. *And* I wouldn't put it past some of the buggers who live in these parts to tell him. To write him letters. They've sod-all to be high and mighty about but they'd bloody soon . . .'

'Get out of here,' said Flensing softly.

'What?'

'Out. On your bike. Blow. Whichever expression meets the case. Just go. I'd like to arrange for this room to be fumigated.'

Ballester found Jumbo Jakeman. It wasn't too difficult; Jakeman had what might be called a "beat"; he spent most of his waking life ambling along a dozen or so streets, going nowhere, coming from nowhere, pausing every few yards to exchange pleasantries

117

or give unwanted advice.

The two detective officers in the unmarked squad car saw the meeting and were puzzled.

'A tip-off?' suggested one in a worried tone.

'Could be,' agreed his companion. 'Our little Andrew is a law unto himself.'

'We're pretty vulnerable. Jakeman doesn't know us, but Ballester does. He even knows this car.'

The second detective lifted the mike from its holder and said, 'When in doubt pass the can.'

The Hallsworth Hill D.D.I. loved rubber plants. The other officers who worked from Hallsworth Hill could take them or leave them. Their lives would not have been warped had they been told they'd never again see a rubber plant. But the D.D.I.? He would have wept. He would have been broken hearted. Which, for a divisional detective inspector, was a little stupid. But no matter. Despite this kinky weakness, he was a good and practical C.I.D. man.

He listened to the detective constable, then pursed his lips into a silent whistle, and said, 'Two hundred and five thousand smackers?'

'And the gun,' added the D.C.

'From biscuit tins in the cock-loft?'

'That's what Innes has told 'em.'

The D.D.I. stood up from his desk chair, strolled to a corner of his office and touched one of the leaves of the rubber plant. Touched it lightly — tenderly — as if caressing the cheek of a loved one.

He said, 'Innes. The North End crowd want him.'

'The Gatling murder,' confirmed the D.C.

'Possible suspect?'

'For questioning.'

'Ah!' The D.D.I. stroked the leaf as he spoke. 'Merely "for questioning". We'll dog-paddle for a little while. Apparently the Met haven't realised who they have in custody.'

'I don't think it was an All Districts message, sir.'

'That's us in the clear, then,' smiled the D.D.I. 'We'll have a session with Joseph Lumb before we contact North End. Then, when the North End crowd build a wall around friend Innes, we have a way in. *We* can join the I-hate-Innes crowd.'

Jimmy Holmes was sure he'd never be warm again. He would have laid money on it. The warmth of the cabs was forgotten. Only the immediate, icy blast which ripped along the station platform was real. It hit his face like a storm of invisible razor blades. It cut deep into the very marrow of his bones and, other than in the buffet, there was no shelter from it.

And the buffet was out. Definitely *out*! What loose change he had left wouldn't run to tea at *that* price. *And* cigarettes. *And* that suspicious look the biddy behind the counter had given him when she'd seen his unshaven, unwashed face.

He'd already stamped along the platform a couple of times, trying to get the circulation going. It hadn't done much good. Only attracted the attention of the fur-coated old cow staring out of the Ladies Waiting Room window. Her eyes had smouldered with disgust as she'd watched him along the full arc of her vision. The sort of rich bitch who might call the railway police and have him shifted.

His two priorities. To get warm and to remain unnoticed. Not a lot, for Christ's sake. Not too much to ask. All he'd done was help dump Sammy's body in a grave. That was all. He hadn't killed him. He hadn't even wanted to cart him to the cemetery. And now, murder. *Murder,* for God's sake! All the weight, all the rank of a full scale murder enquiry. And he, Jimmy Holmes, was on the "wanted for questioning" list. It was like the end of the world. It *was* the end of *his* world. Let the cops get their hands on him and it was going to be a "fix it" job, for sure. Nothing more certain. Innes wouldn't help. Innes would be looking after Number One. And as for Solly. Solly might back him. Why not? Solly hadn't done anything. Like him, Solly had just *been* there. But the cops — y'know — the cops. Call a thing "murder", and they had to have a murderer. The way their minds worked. Call it "murder" and some poor bastard was made to suck the hammer.

When he'd been inside. That six-months stretch. He'd met 'em. G.B.H., unlawful wounding and one bloke in for the big 'un. All fixed. All fitted out by lying cops. The guy in for killing his missus. As innocent as the day was long. Swore to it, with tears in his eyes, he did. Nice chap. No muscle, no aggro, no nothing. Just some poor bastard the cops had fixed. A murder, so there had to be a murderer. Balancing the books. As daft — as lousy — as *that*. So what if he, Jimmy Holmes, *was* innocent? Big deal! He'd be fitted out, then dumped in a dock. That's what.

The only "out" was to keep ducked until they'd tied either Innes or Solly in pink ribbon. Either or both. Then, when the last nail had been driven home, surface and say, 'Who? Me?'

Meanwhile . . .

He found a form, partly sheltered by a stack of mail-bags. He sat down, hoiked the collar of his jacket a little higher, thrust his hands deep into the pockets of his trousers and allowed self-pity to engulf him as he sought, without success, to counter the cold.

Rupert Johnstone, Esq, chief superintendent of police, slipped his folded napkin from its silver ring and placed it geometrically across his lap. His was a mind in which such things were of great importance. The silver napkin ring, the starched linen napkin, the positioning of that napkin, the decanter of red wine (because the basis of the meal was to be roast beef) and the correct glasses. The edge of his table mat was very slightly out of line with the edge of the table, therefore he carefully moved it until it was perfectly true. And, having moved the mat, it was also necessary to re-position the cutlery.

His wife, Christine, wheeled the dumb waiter, complete with hot-plate, from the kitchen. She positioned the dumb waiter within easy reach of Johnstone, plugged the hot-plate into a socket let into the skirting board, then carefully lifted the bowls of vegetables from the dumb waiter and placed them in their exact position on mats spaced about the polished surface of the table.

She sat on a chair, directly opposite her husband's and watched as he picked up the horn-handled knife and steel from alongside the meat dish and drew the blade across the steel in swift, slashing movements, as if each hand was engaging the other in a sabre duel. He returned the steel to its place, picked up the fork and began to slice the beef into wafer-thin portions. The meat was under-cooked, as he liked it, and pink, watery blood followed the cut of the knife and formed a shallow pool in the base of the dish. He apportioned the slices, then visited each dish in turn, scooping out the various vegetables and sharing them between the two plates. Finally he sat back, re-positioned his napkin, clasped his fingers into a double-fist, lowered his head, closed his eyes and muttered, 'For what we are about to receive may the Lord make us duly grateful.'

It was a rigmarole. As meaningless as his habit of checking the time of the electric clock on the mantlepiece with the time of his wrist watch. It was the "done" thing . . . therefore Johnstone *did* it.

They were well into the meal, and Johnstone had poured wine into the two glasses before either of them spoke. a not unusual state of affairs in that, over twenty-three years of marriage, they'd worn what few topics of conversation they had in common to a smooth, uninterested surface.

She murmured, 'How is the murder progressing, my dear?'

'It's not. I doubt if it ever will.'

'Really?' She showed polite surprise.

'Flensing is a difficult man to understand. He rejects friendship, and seems to have no time for discipline.'

'A rod for his own back, surely?' The polite interest remained.

'A truth he'll learn,' Johnstone agreed. 'That, along with the fact that tittle-tattle forms no basis for the detection of crime.'

Thus the tenor of their talk. Boredom wrapped up in words. She asked questions and had no interest whatever in the answers. He gave the answers, along with opinions, knowing that both answers and opinions would be forgotten within minutes of being heard. And yet, had they been asked, they would each have insisted that theirs was a successful marriage. Even a happy marriage. They "belonged" to each other; that is what they would have affirmed. They would have been acutely embarrassed had they been asked whether or not they loved each other, but without hesitation they would have agreed that they "respected" each other. That, for Johnstone and his wife, would have been enough. Stronger emotion than "respect" was something neither understood. They would have scorned the suggestion that no genuinely successful marriage can be built upon mere *respect*; that excitement, that the unexpected and that a mutual love of life counts far more than *respect;* that blazing rows can be the very corner-stones of a magnificent marriage; that to grow together — to become truly "as one" — is a painful and prolonged progress, but the only progress worth a damn.

They were married. They had documented proof of that fact; a certificate which recorded the fact that they were man and wife. But that's *all* they had, and all they would ever have and, to be honest, all they would ever want. They didn't know it, but they were two of the unhappy people of the world.

Towards the end of the meal there was a longer silence than usual.

Christine Johnstone broke it by asking, 'Is he married?'

'Who?'

'Flensing.'

'I — er . . .' Johnstone pondered for a moment, then said, 'I think so. Yes, I'm sure he is. She's an invalid of some sort.'

'An invalid?'

'In hospital, I think.'

'Oh!'

Johnstone lifted his napkin from his lap, dabbed his lips, and said, 'It probably accounts for many things. A thing like that must be rather worrying. Something of a nuisance.'

'Keep away from him,' said Hoyle wearily.

Ballester looked surprised and said, 'Flensing told us to lean on the snouts and Jakeman's one of . . .'

'One of your snouts.' Hoyle ended the sentence for him.

'The one man I can rely on,' said Ballester. 'I've had more good griff from Jakeman than I've had from . . .'

'We're pulling him in, later.' Once more Hoyle stopped the detective sergeant in mid-flow.

'What the hell *for*?'

'Would you believe accessory to murder?'

'Y'mean he had a hand in Gatling's . . .'

'Not Gatling. Another murder. Two — maybe three — years old.'

The look of shocked awe on Ballester's face was almost funny. He'd been surprised, and not a little irritated, when the squad car carrying two uniformed motor patrol officers had drawn up alongside and interrupted his conversation with Jumbo Jakeman. He'd been mollified a little when one of the officers had passed the message that he (Ballester) was required urgently at Lessford D.H.Q. But having hurried to the Murder Room, and been rounded on by Hoyle for almost ruining a surveillance, his annoyance had returned.

And now this.

'*Another* murder?' he gasped.

'Strictly speaking,' said Hoyle, 'Gatling's is the *other* murder. This one's been lying at the bottom for some time. The Gatling enquiry stirred up enough mud for us to spot it.'

'Who?'

'Elsie Manford. Bill Manford's daughter.'

'She left the district — what? — three years back. She . . .'

'That's what everybody thought. What everybody was *meant* to think.'

'Oh!'

'We've had her mother in. Flensing, Adamson and myself. *We've* leaned a little, too. There's not much doubt. Gatling killed her, aided and abetted by your good friend Jumbo Jakeman.'

Ballester said, 'Oh!' again, then sat down on the nearest chair.

'Two hundred and five thousand quid,' said the Hallsworth Hill D.D.I. solemnly. 'Plus a shooter, which I know for a fact you haven't a licence for.'

Honest Joe Lumb didn't feel too honest at the moment. Nor did he feel at ease. A police cell, albeit a police cell with the door wide open, was not the cosiest corner in which to spend a Thursday evening in mid-December. The company, too, could have been improved upon. A detective constable with a zero sense of humour and a minus sign when it came to understanding basic facts of life, and a divisional detective inspector who was obviously enjoying himself in a cart-before-the-horse sort of way. A very physical D.D.I., who *would* insist upon punctuating words with a stomach prod delivered by a stiffened forefinger. Not assualt — by no stretch of the imagination could it be described as a "going over" — nevertheless, Lumb's not inconsiderable belly was already feeling sore and, each time the forefinger shot out to poke exactly the same spot, Lumb winced in anticipation.

'In biscuit tins. In the cock-loft,' continued the D.D.I. 'Bank notes, Lumb my old son. Not rabbits. You don't shove one of each sex in there and wait for a fortune to develop. Money doesn't multiply like that. Two hundred and five thousand came out. Two hundred and five thousand went *in*. Plus a gun. Plus ammunition.' He paused, then added, 'I'm waiting in eager anticipation, old lad.'

'It — they — it wasn't mine,' spluttered Lumb.

'Your house.'

'Oh, aye, but . . . y'know. The old man's. He — he salted it away. Years back.'

'Not bad, for a spur-of-the-moment try,' congratulated the D.D.I.

'It's — it's true. I swear. I didn't know about . . .'

'Your father never lived in that house.' The finger shot out again.

'Don't *do* that,' wailed Lumb.

'What? That?' The forefinger hit the bull's-eye once more.

'For Christ's sake!'

'Who were you going to shoot?' asked the D.D.I. with obvious interest.

'Eh?' Lumb's eyes widened.

'A gun. Ammunition. Who had you lined up?'

'No — for God's sake . . . *no*. Self-protection. That's all. All that money. All that . . .'

'All two hundred and five thousand leaves of lettuce.'

'Aye — well — y'know . . .'

'The picture,' interrupted the D.D.I. 'Joseph Lumb. Every man's friend. The epitome of civic responsibility. Sitting at home with his wife, surrounded by all his hard-earned loot. Then, in comes a thieving hound. Somebody like Reg Innes. A real hard nut who wants to rob poor little Joe of what he's worked for all his life. So . . . what does Joe do? He nips out, gets a step-ladder — something — and forces his gut through the trap-door to the cock-loft. And when he comes back he has a gun. Loaded and ready. Ready to defend his house, his home and his honour.' The finger jabbed home as the D.D.I. added, 'And all this time the thief's taking time off to *watch*?'

'It's — it's not like that. It's . . .'

'Too bloody right it's not like that, old lad. Not at *all* like that. Who had you lined up for a wooden waistcoat?'

'For Christ's sake, *nobody*.'

'It wasn't a toy. It wasn't a cap pistol. It was the real thing, and it shot real bullets.'

'I know,' groaned Lumb. 'It's just that . . .' His fat face creased as he sobbed, 'It was the old man's. I just kept it. That's all.'

'Sentimental value?' The detective constable spoke for the first time. He had a deep voice and the tone was quite expressionless.

'Aye.' Lumb nodded eagerly. 'That's all. For sentimental reasons.'

'Ballocks,' said the D.D.I. cheerfully.

'Look, it's the truth, Mr . . .'

'And the money? Did you keep that for sentimental value?'

'I didn't know how much . . .'

'The hell you didn't know how much.'

'Honest. I never . . .'

'Lumb,' the D.D.I. was suddenly very serious, 'you couldn't be honest if a lie was going to stand you on the drop of York first thing tomorrow morning. You'll die with a lie on your lips, old lad. And when you're introduced to Old Nick the first thing you'll tell him is that you've been straight as a plumb-line. I've been watching you for ages, mate. I've had my hungry, beady little eye on you . . . you wouldn't believe how long. And now I've *got* you. Pink ribbon, fancy wrapping-paper, the lot. And — strictly between these four walls — I'm going to have a ball. I'm not going to throw the book at you. I'm going to throw the whole bloody library.'

'I — I want a solicitor,' gasped Lumb.

'You're entitled to one.' The D.D.I. nodded ponderously. 'You're entitled to telephone for your solicitor this very moment. Unfortunately, we haven't yet had telephones installed in the cells . . . so you'll have to hold your water till *we're* ready.'

Alva Hoyle had a problem. It was (and she would have agreed whole-heartedly) a problem ninety-per-cent of married women would have given their eye-teeth to share. Nevertheless, it *was* a problem.

David, her husband — Detective Chief Inspector Hoyle — loved her more than was good for him. More than was good for both of them.

Nothing physical, you understand. Nothing to do with beds and bedrooms — although that side of their marriage was fine and dandy, thank you very much — but everything to do with learning, knowledge and a general I.Q. factor. Alva had a mind like a dry sponge. It was a gift, a knack, and the Ph.D. had cost her less headwork than the average kid puts into an O level. Nice going, and she wasn't ashamed of her grey matter, but when you're crazy in love with a copper who left school as a merely moderately intelligent teenager silly things crop up and have to be coped with. David had pride. Just about the only weakness she could see in him . . . but it was enough. He was a damn good jack and knew it, but even *that* didn't satisfy. He yearned to match her knowledge, subject for subject and, unlike her, with him it was heavy going. In flash terminology, he was an autodidact, meaning self-taught. More than that even. He was self-taught in his own time; when he should be relaxing and allowing the kinks to straighten themselves from his brain he was burrowing into textbooks on a dozen different disciplines. Never light reading. Never one of those fasten-your-seat-belt-I'm-going-to-tell-everything autobiographies of ageing film and stage personalities written by, or ghosted for, one-time sex-symbols aimed at a public which has already half-forgotten them. For David Hoyle it was always the heavy stuff, even when he waded his way through fiction.

At the moment he was wrestling with Tolstoy's *War and Peace* while, at the same time, munching paté sandwiches and sipping instant coffee.

He sighed, looked up and asked, 'Sweetheart, give me a lead. He flips around. He even changes the names of his characters. He seems to have gone out of his way to *make* it difficult to read.'

She lowered the Simenon, smiled and said, 'Look, my lovely, you're ruining the pleasure of reading.' The hint of sing-song Welsh added to the soothing tone of her voice. 'Tolstoy was an eccentric. Crazy. It's there in the way he writes.'

'The greatest novel ever written.' He raised the heavy book a fraction of an inch as he spoke.

'And there's a load of rubbish.' She placed the Simenon face downwards on the table. 'He wasn't even a *novelist*. Not as we understand that word. A moral teacher, and not even a good one. He was a count. Part of nineteenth-century Russian nobility. My love, he *played* at being socially aware. He couldn't possibly *know*. He released his serfs — freed his slaves — and thought he was doing something great. He was, too. By his yardstick. Slavery — serfdom — as natural to him as breathing. David, my love, when he moves away from dukes and counts — when he writes about *real* people — it shows.'

'It's a great book,' he argued feebly.

'It's a *big* book.' She grinned. 'Try Dostoyevsky. Try *Crime and Punishment* . . . for laughs. There's a book a hard-working copper might enjoy.'

'Talking of coppers.' He lowered the volume and placed it alongside the Simenon. 'Flensing worries me.'

'Tallboy worried you,' she smiled.*

'True.' He pulled a face. 'Maybe *I'm* wrong.'

'Let's say you're *not* wrong.' She reached for a sandwich. 'Let's say you've cause to be worried. Why?'

'He's a . . .' He closed his mouth and sought for better words. 'Like a mechanical shovel. He shifts *everything*. Nothing specific. He digs the lot up.'

'You'd prefer a scalpel approach?' She bit into the sandwich.

'Yeah . . . I suppose.' He didn't sound sure.

'My lovely.' She chewed, then swallowed. 'His job — *your* job — to turn stones and see what tries to scurry away. Not just to net nice little sticklebacks.'

'So it's *me* that's wrong?'

'David, my love, you're a purist,' she said gently. 'You're both *right*. Equally right. Equally necessary. Flensing digs into the dross and finds the uncut diamond. You polish it into a gem stone. You each need the other.'

'You make him sound like a navvy,' he grunted.

'No. *You* make him sound like a navvy. *I* see him as the man who organises the original spade-work.'

'Maybe.' There was a hint of petulance in the half-admission. He reached for the last sandwich on the plate. 'All I know is, he takes a suspicious death, jumps in with both feet and calls it murder . . .'

'Which it may well be. Probably is.'

'. . . then sends the whole team on a gossip-hunt, and ends up with what might be a *second* murder.'

'A glutton for punishment.' Her eye twinkled as she added, 'That makes two of you.'

A thought struck him and he said, 'You seem to know him.'

'Of him,' she admitted.

'How? You've never met him. How do you know so much . . .'

---

*See Anatomy of a Riot, Macmillan London, 1982

127

'The hospital, my love.' The teasing left her eyes and was replaced by gentle sorrow. 'I've met his wife. We talk whenever we can. Bobbies wives, you know. She's a great woman. She deserves a good man.'

Helen Flensing said, 'If he's half as good a man as his wife thinks he is, you'll make a good team.'

'He's good,' smiled Flensing. 'He's *very* good.'

The men with whom Flensing worked would not have recognised him. He was alive. His voice was no longer the drawling monotone they knew. Even his stance — the movement of his body — conveyed a vitality rooted in the near proximity of the person for whom he existed.

Helen Flensing knew all this and marvelled that it was so. What had they other than memories? Great memories, magnificent memories but, for all that, only memories.

She said, 'Credit him with it, Ralph. It will mean a lot.'

'Don't I always?'

'No, you do *not*. I hear too many tales.'

'This time, I promise,' he said gently.

That this husband of hers — that *any* man — could have such compassion. Such understanding. Such absolute loyalty. She could never get used to it. Never even understand it. He was, without doubt, the absolute in the one-woman-one-man field.

He said, 'Not a long visit this time, darling. Tomorrow I'll try to make it a little longer.'

'Please.'

'The villains of the world have to be kept in order.'

He bent and kissed her on the lips, and it was no token gesture. The love was there — the depth and passion he'd always felt. She could tell. It was something beyond the possibility of make-believe.

She watched his reflection through the mirror as he walked from the tiny ward and, for the thousandth time, she cursed the damned injury which imprisoned her in the iron lung.

FIVE

The drop in temperature brought a night mist. Years back, before a percentage of muck was legally removed from the atmosphere, it would have been a pre-Christmas pea-souper; something to stir the pen of a latter-day Dickens or a would-be Conan Doyle; something to make the less literary-inclined hawk and spit and curse the filth being forced into their suffering lungs. As it was, it merely brought the shivers. It crept down collars and up capes. It mocked warm clothes and stroked well-covered skin with icy fingers. It effectively removed all joyful anticipation of the forthcoming Yuletide; those on the street — coppers and civilians alike — saw their breath billowing in front of their faces and wondered how in hell's name they were going to crawl through one more winter.

In the main room of The Bunch of Grapes it was moderately warm. Thursday night was one of the slack periods, nevertheless the radiators cracked as they tried to obey the thermostat, pipe and cigarette smoke built up to blanket-thickness and the booze and big-talk brought temporary forgetfulness of what was beyond the swing-doored exit. Quince was with the customers, shooting off his mouth. His wife was alone behind the bar — Edwina Manford hadn't shown up to help pull pints and measure shorts — but the custom was such that she wasn't rushed off her feet.

Quince was one of a trio sharing a corner table alongside one of the radiators. His companions were a short man, with a distinct squint in his right eye and dirty finger-nails, and Jumbo Jakeman. Each was trying to out-lie the other two.

'I seen it with my own eyes,' Jakeman was saying in his thick, adenoidal voice. 'Big as a cat, it was. I never seen a bigger rat in my life. And he picked it up, bit into its neck and it was as dead as a nit.'

'Those old rat-catchers,' mused squint-eye.

'Break its neck, did he?' asked Quince.

'Naw.' Jakeman shook his head, then sipped his beer. 'There's a vein there, see? Those old rat-men had good teeth. Bite into the vein, spit out the blood . . . that's it.'

'I once saw a rat,' said squint-eye dreamily. 'Years back. Leeds market. Up in the roof on the steel girders. Two-foot long, if it was an inch. Not counting the tail. Christ! Talk about panic. Market-day, it was. Everybody standing there watching the bloody thing.'

The door opened and Ballester entered. He glanced round the room, spotted the trio and walked across.

'They tell me . . .' Quince closed his mouth as Ballester arrived at the table.

'Jakeman,' growled Ballester.

Quince scowled and said, 'What is it this time? Can't you people leave this place . . .'

'Stuff it, Quince.' Ballester jerked his head and repeated, 'Jakeman.'

'Something you wanted, Mr Ballester?' asked Jakeman.

'Aye. You.'

The other customers were watching. At the best of times Ballester was short-weighted on tact and having, as he saw it, been made a monkey of by Jakeman, he saw no reason whatever to hide his natural aggression. Quince, on the other hand, had had a gutful of coppers for one day; the custom he catered for weren't too keen on fuzz suddenly arriving and making for general discomfort all round.

'Look . . .' he began.

'Why? What is there to see?' snapped Ballester.

'You can't . . .'

'I bloody *can*. And unless you've got a Panzer division hiding up the back of your coat, you'd better keep quiet.'

Even for Ballester this was going some. He was winding himself up for a once-in-a-lifetime set-to. Quince had enough sense to recognise the promise of real trouble. His jaw muscles twitched, his nostrils flared and the blood drained from his face, but he obediently kept quiet.

Jakeman pushed himself away from the table and edged awkwardly towards Ballester. He, too, looked puzzled and uncertain. Ballester was his tame cop; the personal spring from which Newcastle Brown flowed whenever he (Jakeman) spoke the magic words. Why, only today . . .

'Move it!' rapped Ballester.

'Mr Ballester, I don't know what . . .'

'You'd better be a bloody good guesser.' Ballester's fingers

132

clamped themselves on Jakeman's arm, just above the elbow. Hard enough to hurt. Hard enough to leave tiny bruises. 'Between here and the nick, you'd better guess right.'

The weather was no less bleak, no less miserable, in Birmingham. Even the shelter of the general waiting room gave scant relief from the energy-sapping cold.

Not that Jimmy Holmes had much energy left to sap. He was becoming befuddled. He wasn't quite sure how long it was since he last slept; how many days, how many nights, since he'd last crawled from his bed. Even eating — a real meal — when, for Christ's sake? The stubble on his chin, the grime on his face, his uncombed and matted hair. He was no Beau Brummel, but even *he* had limits and he felt distinctly itchy for want of a good scrub down.

He lighted another cigarette and the smoke touched his already parched throat and brought on a fit of coughing loud enough to make the few other occupants of the room glance at him with added distaste.

Not that he gave a damn. Not that he gave a damn about anything any more. He had a wife somewhere . . . or had he? He had kids . . . or had he? *Was* there a place called Lessford? *Did* men called Solly Daniels and Reg Innes exist? *Had* a fool called Sammy Gatling made an idiotic call during a game of solo whist? And if so, when? And where? And why? And . . .

'Now then, lad.'

Holmes raised his red-rimmed eyes and peered, short-sightedly, at the uniformed giant standing in front of him. Nothing registered for a moment and he screwed up his face in an effort of concentration.

'You're not travelling,' said the British Rail constable in a voice which was neither loud nor aggressive. It was a simple statement of fact and not open to argument. 'This place is for people waiting for trains.'

'Eh?' Holmes fought to understand what was being said to him.

'What's your name, son?'

'Holmes.'

It was out without thought. One of the few questions Holmes was still capable of answering without having to batter his swirling brain.

The constable peered more closely at the unshaven, grubby

face, then said, 'From Lessford?'

Holmes nodded.

'Come on, lad.' The constable held out a hand; a kindly enough hand, which matched the solemn compassion in his voice. 'Let's have you somewhere warm. Clean you up a bit, and get some grub in your guts.'

In many ways it was rather like the children's game of Passing the Parcel, but in reverse. Innes was the parcel and, rather than passing him, everybody wanted to grab him.

The Hallsworth Hill D.D.I. said, 'We've nailed him for nicking more than two-hundred thousand in cash and kind from this division. I think we should have first bite.'

The D Division inspector said, 'Sorry, mate. We *have* him and it's attempted murder . . . whatever it ends as.'

The Hallsworth Hill D.D.I. argued half-heartedly, then hung up before telephoning North End Division.

Inspector King said, 'Why in hell's name didn't you let us know before?'

'Verification, old lad. Didn't want to go off at half-cock. Anyway, that's where he is. Let me know when you've collected him. We'd like words with him about a break-in he committed before he hot-footed it south.'

King telephoned D Division and said, 'Suspected murder. It's important we get him up here.'

'*Suspected* murder. That's not a criminal offence mate. *Attempted* murder. That is.'

'We need to question him.'

'Tell us the questions, mate. We'll ask.'

'Look, I'd rather . . .'

'We know *how* to ask questions.'

'All right.' King capitulated with a sigh. 'It's about the death of Samuel Gatling.'

The conversation lasted about fifteen minutes. Copper-talk, which meant copper-shorthand. In one way it was King's manner of testing the capability of the unkown Met man, although it was done by King without conscious thought. The phraseology. The slang. The short-sentenced under-statement. Something not taught at police colleges; something only learned by years of practical policing. The inspector from D Division passed with

134

flying colours, and gradually King accepted the situation. Innes was going to be made to jump through all the proper hoops . . . without even touching the sides.

Ballester opened the door of Number One Interview Room, then knocked the light switch <u>down</u> with one hand, while at the same time he placed the palm of the other hand between Jakeman's shoulder blades and pushed as hard as possible. The neon strips flickered, then held, and Jakeman stumbled forward, caught the top of his shins against the edge of one of the tubular chairs, then sprawled on the floor. Ballester slammed the door shut, stepped towards the fallen Jakeman and Jakeman knew he was in for hard trouble.

'Up!' snarled Ballester.

'For Christ's sake, what am I supposed to have . . .'

'On your feet, you miserable tow-rag. Or do you want me to *kick* your teeth down your throat.'

'You — you can't . . .'

'Don't bet on it, Jakeman. Don't bet on *anything*. This is a very dangerous place. Some nasty accidents have happened in this room.'

Jakeman hauled himself upright then, gingerly watching Ballester's reaction, lowered himself onto one of the chairs.

There was fear in that room; fear amounting to blind terror. Jakeman was from a class brought up to believe that the police, and especially detectives, could get away with anything up to, and including, maiming; that, regardless of what physical violence Ballester indulged in, there could be no redress, because the courts were mere extensions of the general system of "law enforcement", there to provide official justification for all outrages. As a child he'd been quietened by the threat of "telling the bobbies" whenever he'd cried. As a young teenager he had, on two occasions, been dragged to the nearest police station by an angry father and there, thanks to the co-operation of a long-retired sergeant, been locked in a police cell overnight for no other reason than to frighten him into curbing youthful mischief. Sure, he'd been a "problem child". Sure, he'd grown into a "juvenile delinquent". But long before that the stratum of society in which he'd lived had planted the firm belief that policemen — "the scum", "the nickers", "the shit", "the fuzz"

135

— were, to a man, an enemy to be feared, outwitted if possible, but never trusted.

Strangely, Ballester was the reverse side of the same coin. Big as a youth, he was a born bully. Aggression was his strong point, and in the world in which he'd lived, aggression or threat of aggression had always paid off. An only child, and a spoiled brat, he'd grown to believe that to ask was to receive and, if the giving wasn't immediate, he had muscles to implement the request. A hard and sullen man, his marital troubles had soured him into little more than an official thug but, like all such men, he didn't recognise himself for what he was. In his own eyes he was part of a shield there to keep anarchy at bay; an over-worked, battle-scarred warrior who'd been tricked by one of the opposition and whose sworn duty it was to bring that smart bastard to heel and make damn sure he paid, full weight, for past sins.

He leaned forward and down until his eyes were less than six inches from Jakeman's face, then snarled, 'Don't arse me around, Jakeman. Be warned . . . don't arse me around.'

'I — I'm not. I wouldn't . . .'

'Back a few years. To Elsie Manford.'

'I — I dunno what . . .'

'To when she was murdered. You had a hand in it, Jakeman. You and Gatling. Gatling's dead. You're not, but start spinning the fanny and you'll wish you bloody-well were. Talk, you miserable, mis-shapen git. Talk and keep talking.'

Jakeman's eyes widened and he gasped, 'For Christ's sake, no! I didn't have anything to do with . . .'

Ballester's fist was as tight and hard as a cricket ball. It travelled less than a foot, but it had muscle behind it and it was still gathering speed when it landed above and to one side of Jakeman's groin. Jakeman's jaw dropped as the pain hit him. From the back of his throat came a thin keen of agony as he folded from the chair and slipped to the floor of Number One Interview Room.

'Where's May?' asked Adamson.

'Out at a disco . . . I think.' Kath glanced up from the cookery book she was consulting, then added, 'With Wallace.'

'Who's Wallace?'

'Her boy friend.' Kath touched the cookery book and

continued, 'Cinnamon cakes. What do you think? They'll make a change from Christmas cake when people pop in unexpectedly.'

'This is a bit . . .'

'Do you think they'll go with sherry? Or whisky? They'll be fine with coffee, but . . .'

'This is news to me.'

'What? Cinnamon cakes? We used to have them . . .'

'No. This "boy friend" business.'

They were in the kitchen. It was cosy; the heat from the <u>central-heating boiler</u> gave off a comfortable warmth and, until that moment, Adamson had been standing with his rump against the white enamel of the boiler surround, sipping tea, munching home-made drop cakes, watching his wife plan even more goodies for the coming weeks and figuring what a lucky guy he was, prior to donning outdoor clothes and setting off for another stint on duty with Hoyle. The sudden turn of conversation made him push himself away from the boiler. His expression showed surprise, almost amounting to shock, coupled with worry.

Kath looked puzzled and said, 'What's wrong?'

'I . . .' Adamson moved the hand holding the beaker in a vague gesture of non-understanding.

'She's out at a disco,' said Kath. 'Kids do, these days. They don't go to the cinema as often as we did.'

'That's not what . . .' Adamson moistened his lips. 'This Wallace character? Is that his first name?'

'Of course.' Kath nodded.

'There's no "of course" about it. Who is he?'

'Wallace, that's all I know. He goes to the same school as May.'

'You said something about "boy friend".'

'Yes.' Again, Kath nodded. 'He called for her a couple of hours ago.'

'Just like that?' The worry and surprise were turning to anger.

'What's wrong?' Now Kath looked surprised. 'What're all the storm clouds about?'

'Don't you damn-well *care*?' he snapped.

'Don't I . . .'

'Some young pup calls and takes her out. God knows where . . .'

'They're at the disco.'

'God only knows what they're up to, and . . .'

'They're dancing. Drinking Coke.' She held onto her own rising temper, and forced a half-smile. 'Probably feeling very naughty and smoking a cigarette.'

'For God's sake woman . . .'

'Don't "woman" me!' she flared. 'I'm not some tart you're interviewing. I'm not some . . .'

'Sorry. Sorry.' He looked crestfallen, and her own anger dissipated as quickly as it had boiled. He muttered, 'She's only a kid. They don't have "boy friends" at her age. They're not . . .'

'She's what we made her,' she said gently. She touched his arm, smiled and said, 'They're *both* kids. Peter . . . don't have a dirty mind.'

He stammered, 'No. It's not that I . . .'

'It is, and you know it.'

'But, y'know, a "boy friend", at her age.'

'All right. Her *friend* . . . who just happens to be a boy of about her own age.'

'Same thing, surely?' he growled.

'No.' She sighed and looked at this man of hers, who was so secretly unsure of himself. Patiently, she explained, 'She's not in a convent, darling. We wouldn't want her to be. She lives in the world. The *real* world. To you it's a pretty rotten world. But that's because of your job. To me it's a very comfortable, very sure world. And that's because of you, and May, and I've sense enough to know how lucky I am. But to her it is still a very *new* world. A happy and exciting world, with lots of noise and new experiences . . .'

'That's what scares me.'

'What?'

'Those — y'know — "experiences" she might try.'

'She's our daughter. Our child.' She was suddenly very serious. 'I've taught her. Told her. Explained things. I've done what I thought was my duty . . .'

'I'm not suggesting . . .'

'She knows all about sex and babies.'

'Oh!'

'When it's right. *And* when it's wrong. More important, we've both set her an example.' She paused, then continued, 'If you must look at it that way, this is the test. This period of her life.

138

If we've been good parents, we've nothing to worry about. If she goes wrong, It's not just her fault. It's our fault, too. But don't worry — I'm not worrying — she *won't* go wrong. She's too much of you in her.'

Adamson stared at the tiled floor of the kitchen. For the moment, he couldn't speak; daren't trust himself to speak. The shock had turned to anger, and now the anger had turned to a strange, choking shame. So easy to be a bastard, eh? So easy not to give a damn. But try being decent, mate. Try falling in love and staying in love. Try *that* for size. Nice. More than nice. Bloody wonderful. But not easy. Painful sometimes. *Bloody* painful. Times were, it could tear your guts out. Rip your heart from its moorings. Fill you so full, you could hardly breathe. In this life you pay for everything, and what you don't pay for you don't get, but by Christ . . .

Kath came close and kissed him on the cheek.

She whispered, 'Buck up, darling. She's a smasher, and nobody will ever be good enough for her. But there's a few years before *that* happens.'

King thought he'd heard somebody walk along the corridor. Stumble along the corridor really. Making for the interview rooms. For Number One Interview Room at a guess. Maybe David Hoyle. Maybe Flensing. He felt he should check; make sure everything was up-to-the-minute. He left the Murder Room, walked along the corridor and raised a hand to knock on the door of Number One Interview Room. He didn't knock. Instead he stood motionless, listening to the sound of whimpering coming from inside the room. Mewing noises, as if from some animal in prolonged pain. Without knocking he opened the door.

Jakeman was curled up on the floor, holding his guts and moaning gently to himself; he was unmarked about the face, but his eyes were screwed tight against the pain and in anticipation of Ballester's already raised shoe.

'Hold it!' King shouted the words as he catapulted himself into the interview room. He grabbed Ballester by a shoulder and threw him against the wall. Ballester, caught one-footed, almost fell then hit the wall and pushed himself upright. For a moment he looked as if he might launch himself at the inspector. King yelled, '*Don't*. My God, I'll cripple you if you even try.'

139

'What the bloody hell . . .'

'Shut up. You're nicked.'

'Don't talk like a sodding . . .'

'Nicked. I'll read the damn caution at you, if that's what you want.'

They were shouting at each other. They hated each other and, for the moment, all else was forgotten.

Jakeman had opened his eyes. He stayed on the floor, still curled in a foetal position and still holding his middle with both arms. His face was ashen and twisted with pain and the faint sheen of sweat polished the skin.

He gasped, 'Mister . . .'

'Stay where you are,' snapped King. He strode to the door and bawled, 'Sergeant Lowe!'

They stood waiting. King and Ballester panting; Jakeman watching from the floor and making quick, whimpering noises as the pain continued. Lowe arrived and stopped as if he'd hit an invisible wall.

'What the . . .' he began.

'Ballester. Lock him up.' King jerked a thumb. 'G.B.H. Charge him. Show me as the arresting officer.'

Ballester snarled, 'You're bloody mad. You can't . . .'

'Do it, sergeant,' snapped King.

Lowe hesitated and said, 'Look, sir, don't you think . . .'

'That's an order, Sergeant Lowe. Search him, charge him, lock him away in a cell. Now!'

'Yes, sir.'

'But first get an ambulance.' King glanced at the curled up form of Jakeman. 'Get this one to hospital. I think he's badly injured.'

'Yes, sir.' Lowe looked sad. Perhaps a little uncertain. This situation wasn't covered by any book of words. A villain like Jakeman. A fellow-copper — fellow-sergeant — albeit one a mite on the mad side. If sides *had* to be taken . . . He sighed and repeated, 'Yes, sir.'

As he turned to return to the Murder Room, King added, 'And don't waste time apologising.'

William Manford.

The criminologists, the penologists and all the other "ologists" who make great play around understanding the workings of the criminal mind and the after-effects of prolonged confinement in H.M. prisons know little, or nothing, about the William Manfords of the world. To these people Bill Manford was a success. *Their* success. He'd been "rehabilitated". After long stretches in jail he'd at last seen the light — the error of his ways — and was a good and upright citizen.

The truth? Bill Manford had once been wild, but now he was trained. Trained . . . not tamed. Nobody can take a tiger from its jumgle and *tame* it. The most they can do is *train* it. It remains a tiger and, beneath the striped skin, the muscles still ripple; the claws and teeth are as sharp as ever; even beyond the darkness of that jungle night, the light still burns as brightly as ever . . . it is merely shaded.

So, with Bill Manford and his breed. He'd been hammered into a kind of submission. The cops had hammered him, the courts had hammered him, the screws had hammered him. Most of all the world — the only world he knew — had hammered him. "Cell-happy". "Stir-crazy". A dozen different flash ways of putting it. The truth was he'd fought himself to a standstill. The punishment he'd absorbed, while trying to live his life *his* way, had resulted in a kind of silent punch-drunkenness.

He worked for the local water authority. He dug holes and trenches, then filled them in. Pushed by the after-care people, the water authority had been doubtful about employing him, but already he was counted as a prize. He worked without let-up; steadily, grimly, never stopping and never moving beyond or below the same rhythmic pace. He rarely spoke, rarely smiled and his stern-faced manner kept his fellow-workers at arm's-length. He'd been required to join a union, and he'd joined, but only once had the local shop steward approached him to deliver a mild pep-talk. The cold eyes had stared into the official's face for a moment, then the swing of the pick and the arc of the shovel had continued. The pick had slammed into the ground less than an inch from the shop steward's boot, and at that point the official had received the message, loud and clear. Manford was a member . . . period. Too many pip-squeaks had already ordered him around, and the next swing of the pick was going to pin the shop steward's foot to the ground. The shop steward had grunted, 'Well — tha knows . . .' left it at that and moved hurriedly

141

beyond range.

"Love". "Christmas". "Good Tidings and Great Joy". What the hell did those words and phrases mean? Bill Manford didn't know. He had no yardstick via which to measure them. Some people he scorned more than others. A handful — but very few — had earned his grudging respect, but as for *love*. That, mate, was a non-existent commodity, hawked by con-merchants in the pages of cheap magazines. Something women dreamed about, and as real as Cinderella's glass slipper. A bloody fairy tale. An act — a come-on, a routine — geared to grab what little pride the bastards had left you, and rob you even of *that*.

That was Bill Manford. The "success". The "rehabilitated criminal". A compact bundle of seething bitterness and silent rage.

Flensing, Hoyle and Adamson arrived at the Murder Room within minutes of each other. Flensing, the first to arrive, saw the ambulance pull away from Lessford D.H.Q. and race away with lights flashing and siren wailing. King broke the news. His voice was tight and harsh with residual anger, and his face still flushed with emotion.

'Jakeman,' grunted Adamson. 'As bent as a drunk's handwriting.'

'Constable,' snapped King, 'I don't give a damn if he's Charlie Peace, Ballester had no right to . . .'

'He's snapped the chain.' Flensing drawled the interruption. The half-closed eyes and weary expression masked whatever feelings he had. 'Jakeman. Then we might have been ready to flick a few warm questions Manford's way.' He turned to Adamson and asked, 'Manford? Is he open to kidology?'

'He's heard it all before, sir,' sighed Adamson. 'On the other hand, he seems to have straightened himself out.'

'Assuming he walked in here, this minute,' murmured Flensing. 'Assuming he casually mentioned *he'd* smacked Gatling across the skull. Would we need smelling salts to bring *you* round?'

'No, sir.' Adamson didn't hesitate.

'Something,' muttered Hoyle.

King said, 'We bring him in?' and made it half-question, half-suggestion.

142

'We control our bladders, inspector,' said Flensing. 'Hopefully, we've started the boat rocking. His better three-quarters was mildly shattered when she left. She'll still be jittery.'

'She'll be at The Bunch of Grapes,' said Hoyle.

King added, 'That was about the death of their daughter though, wasn't it?'

'Elsie Manford,' said Flensing dreamily. 'Samuel Gatling. If we're right, one led to the other.'

Adamson said, 'The Cutters didn't have much doubt.'

'Therefore,' said Flensing, 'we've started waves. Quince hasn't much oil left to pour on the troubled waters . . .'

'Quince,' grunted Hoyle, 'is feeling very queazy himself.'

'Therefore, we give it time. Let it build up into something of a storm. The possible scenario? Mrs Manford dithers. Quince doesn't help matters. Manford has a suspicious mind. Things are said. What is laughingly called a "domestic disturbance" ensues. I think — what? — three o'clock in the morning might be a good time. Hard feelings all round. We knock on the door, if they're in bed disturb their troubled sleep. Add a few drops of subtle poison and hope the brew boils over.' Without change of tone or expression, he went on, 'We're bad bastards, gentlemen. We do wicked things. If we do them well enough we stand a fifty-fifty chance of plucking a pearl or two from the mess we cause. By the way is Manford still under surveillance?'

King said, 'Yes, sir,' then added, 'the two lunatics keeping an eye on Jakeman could have stopped all this nonsense.'

'Ballester out-ranked them,' said Hoyle.

'Nevertheless . . .'

'That horse has already bolted,' murmured Flensing. 'Let the door swing on its hinges.'

King was about to say something else, but the telephone bell beat him to it. He strode three steps, lifted the receiver and, as they listened to one half of a telephone conversation, the other three saw some of the darkness lift from King's expression. He even managed a smile which matched the outside weather.

He replaced the receiver, walked back to the group, and said, 'Holmes is inside. Birmingham Railway Police picked him up at the station.'

Flensing nodded his satisfaction.

In a more sardonic tone, King continued, 'He hasn't committed any known offences. No murder. No attempted murder. He's awaiting collection.'

'Good.' Flensing moved his glance between the two inspectors. 'Any volunteers for the journey?'

'I'll go,' said King, then added, 'That is, if David doesn't mind taking over this place.'

'I have till three in the morning,' smiled Hoyle.

Flensing said, 'A squad car. Two drivers. They can spell each other. Straight there, straight back. Oh, and — er — caution him before you start for home. If he gets bored he might sing you a few choruses of some popular songs.'

'I'll listen for the words,' promised King.

Adamson said, 'I'll let his wife know. She might be worrying.'

Flensing murmured, 'Believe in more likely miracles, constable. But tell her. She can see him after six, if she can hold out that long.'

Lowe went through the rigmarole. Caution; charge; search; the arrest report; the charge sheet; the property listing; the acceptance of Ballester's shoes, belt and tie. It was done methodically but, apart from an occasional grunt, in silence.

Having bagged the final item and completed the final form, he said, 'That's it then. You know the way to the cells.'

'He must be bloody mad,' said Ballester harshly.

'Somebody is,' agreed Lowe.

'You mean you . . .'

'I mean you were always too handy with your weight, mate,' said Lowe sadly. 'You've dropped yourself in the biggest load of manure you could find, and all for the sake of a pillock like Jakeman.'

'He had it coming.'

'Had he?' Lowe nodded towards the door leading to the cell area.

'Anybody but King and . . .'

'No!' Lowe was suddenly very angry. 'Not just King. Anybody. I saw what you'd done, remember? Not just a quick backhander. He wasn't acting it up. It wasn't a put-on. What the hell you hit him with, it did damage. Real damage. The bloody newspapers will get it. Headlines. Questions in Parliament. Home Office enquiries. Christ knows what else. We'll all get stick for that little lot, mate. The whole force. Your lot don't wear uniform. You walk down the street — on duty or not — who the hell knows you? But *us*. The lads with buttons. Everybody knows *us*. Every flaming motorist who drives like a maniac. Every drunk, every yob, every tart hawking her mutton. *We'll* take the slang for what you did tonight. We'll be the rotten bastards. The Gestapo. Whatever name they care to think up. *Us* . . . not the bloody C.I.D.' Lowe caught his rising temper, then growled, 'I'm glad it was a uniformed man who nicked you, Ballester. At least, we can say *that*. Now — last time of asking — start moving towards that cell. You're at the wrong end of the plank, mate. And you're not the only man with hands.'

The inspector from D Division was a difficult man to convince. *His* manor housed a fair scattering of *real* villians; not (in the considered opinion of the inspector from D Division) glorified hayseeds fresh out of the nearest corn field. Men like "Scarface Jock" Russo, the Richardsons, the Krays *and* worse walked the streets of the Big City, and D Division, like every other division in the Met, had hole-outs and rat holes in which they lived or gathered and which had to be kept flushed out and deodorised in order to prevent the germs from spreading. The interview, therefore, bordered upon a slightly off-beat comedy.

'They tell me you murdered somebody up in Lessford.'

'Bloody hell, you can't . . .'

The sergeant, who made up the trio, stepped across the room to the seated Innes, rapped him smartly on top of the skull with the knuckle of a bent finger and said, 'No swearing, sonny. We can. You can't.'

'I didn't murder anybody,' wailed Innes. 'I didn't . . .'

'Somebody called Gatling,' said the inspector.

'I keep telling you. I didn't even . . .'

'Samuel Gatling.'

'Aye. I know him — *knew* him — but . . .'

'You murdered him.'

'Like hell I . . . Christ. don't *do* that,' pleaded Innes, as the knuckle found its mark again. 'It *hurts*.'

'That's why I do it,' said the sergeant flatly.

The inspector said, 'Hit him accros the back of the head with a blunt instrument.'

145

'Hey, you can't . . .' For one awful moment, Innes thought the inspector was giving instructions to the sergeant. Then he swallowed and said, 'Who?'

'Gatling.'

'What?'

'Hit him across the back of the head with a blunt instrument,' the inspector repeated patiently. 'Croaked him.'

'Who? *Me*?' Innes's eyes popped.

'Not *him*.' The inspector glanced at the sergeant.

'That's — that's bl . . . That's *mad*.' Innes stopped the forbidden word just in time.

'Wrapped him up in a sheet. Dumped him in a grave. All neat and proper.'

'Look, mister, I dunno where you get all this . . .'

'From men I'm inclined to believe.'

'They've — they've got it all . . .'

'Not from snivelling, lying little sods who try to shoot people.'

'Eh?'

'Like you.'

'Look, I didn't . . .'

'You *did*. He'll have to sprawl on his belly for weeks.'

'Is it an addiction?' asked the sergeant without much interest.

'What?'

'Killing people.'

'What the bloody hell . . . Jesus Christ, don't *do* that.'

'Watch your language.'

The inspector said, 'Blunt instruments. Guns. You don't care what you use, do you?'

'I haven't killed anybody,' said Innes tearfully.

'Gatling?'

'No. I didn't . . .'

'He's dead.'

'I — I know, but . . .'

'*Somebody* killed him.'

'No. He wasn't . . .'

'You mean he's still alive?'

'No. He's dead. But . . .'

'Meaning you *did* kill him?'

'No. I *didn't*.'

'You were there.'

146

'Yes, I know. But . . .'

'Somebody else killed him?'

'Well — not exactly . . .'

'While you watched?'

'No.' Innes blinked, then whispered. 'I — I pushed him.'

'Eh?'

'That's all.'

'I didn't hear.'

'I pushed him,' said Innes in a slightly louder voice.

'With a blunt instrument?'

'Eh? No. With . . .'

'Across the back of the skull?'

'No. Please . . . *no!* On the chest. That's all.'

'That's clever.'

'W-what is?'

'Pushing somebody in the chest and giving him a fractured skull.'

'No. I didn't.'

'Push him in the chest?'

'Yes, I pushed him in the chest.'

'And fractured his skull?'

'N-no . . . I . . .'

'*Somebody* fractured his skull.'

'Yes, I know. But . . .'

'Who?'

'Well — nobody, really.'

'You just said somebody *did*.'

'No. I didn't mean . . .'

'Innes, fractured skulls don't come under the heading of "optical illusions".'

'No. I know. But . . .'

'This Gatling character died from a fractured skull.'

'Yes, I know.'

'Somebody fractured it.'

'Yes, I know.'

'You?'

'No . . . not really.'

Very solemnly, the inspector said, 'I think you're feeling the weight.'

'Eh?'

'Of this thing.'

'How d'you mean?'

'Feeling the weight. On your mind. On your conscience. On your thoughts. On your balls, for all I know. But feeling the weight.'

'You — you won't fix me?' said Innes in a tiny voice.

'Fix you? What's he talking about sergeant?'

The sergeant said, 'It's a new expression to me.'

'Oh, for God's sake!' groaned Innes.

'He isn't here at the moment.'

'Who?'

'God. Just us three.'

'If — if I tell you the truth.'

'That'll be something of a novelty.'

'No — honest . . . I want to be honest,' pleaded Innes.

'Would you know how?'

'I — I want to tell the truth.'

'Feel free.'

'You — you won't believe me.'

'Ah!'

'Will you?'

'You mean me? Us? Or the people up in Lessford?'

'Anybody,' groaned Innes.

'Will we believe him, sergeant?'

'We always believe the truth, sir.'

'Y'see?' The inspector smiled. 'If it *is* the truth. Then we believe it. Otherwise . . .'

Lessford Royal Infirmary counted Alva Hoyle as something of a snip. She came under the heading of "part-time auxiliary staff", but that was only because officialdom had to call her *something*. She sported a Ph.D, therefore she was a "doctor" in her own right. As for her duties? They were unspecified and all-embracing. Equally, she would sluice out the bed-pans or sit ready to comfort a patient just in from the operating theatres, wheel round the tea trolley or lend a helping hand at the booking in and out desk. At a pinch she could ease the weight a little at an over-worked pharmacy. She was unpaid, cheerful and willing to do anything to help keep the great citadel of suffering ticking over as smoothly as possible. She was very popular. Even the union militants had been won over; the hell she was providing cheap labour, she was never on one job long enough to do other than assist the professionals and, despite her own depth of learning, she never jibed at following instructions.

Her husband, Detective Chief Inspector Hoyle was going to be on duty all night so, because she rarely needed more than four hours' sleep each night, she'd climbed into her Mini, driven to the Infirmary and sought out odd jobs which needed doing. A spell wrapping tiny gifts in Christmas paper. Ten minutes in a darkened ward holding the hand of a middle-aged man who thought he was dying . . . and probably was. Straightening the blankets and trolleys after the nightly influx of injured drunks and accident cases at the Emergency Wards. Spelling a porter on the switchboard while he trotted off to say "Goodnight" to his daughter who was in with a broken thigh.

And now, holding two mugs of hot drinking chocolate in one hand, she opened the door of the tiny ward, allowed the spring to close the door behind her and in a soft voice said, 'Helen.'

From the gloom, Helen Flensing's greeting held real pleasure.

'Alva, pet. How nice of you to drop in.'

'Strictly against rules and regulations.' Alva placed one of the mugs within easy reach of Helen then, seeing the headphones draped around Helen's neck, she said, 'Sorry. Am I interrupting something?'

'Some naturalist.' Helen eased the headphones from her neck, draped them over their peg and flicked a toggle to "off". 'How earwigs copulate . . . along those lines.'

'Very interesting,' grinned Alva.

'For earwigs,' agreed Helen. She reached for the mug, sipped, then asked, 'How are the men doing?'

'Mine,' said Alva solemnly, 'is floundering through *War and Peace*.'

'Good Lord! And I sometimes find Hemingway hard going.'

'He sometimes is.' Then, in answer to the real question, 'I think they're bogged down. But of course David won't admit it.'

'They never will,' agreed Helen. 'Men — especially policemen — a very mulish breed.'

'Especially detectives.'

As if on impulse, Helen said, 'Why did you marry him?' Then, hurriedly, 'No! It's none of my business. I'm sorry. I shouldn't

149

have asked.'

'Swaps?' smiled Alva.

Helen turned her head slightly and looked puzzled.

Alva said, 'I'll tell *you*, if you'll tell me.'

'Agreed.' Helen returned the smile. 'Let's be all girls together. Really catty.'

'Well now,' Alva thought for a moment, tasted the chocolate, then mused, 'I go for hands. Odd, that. With some women it's hair. Blonde, Aryan-type stuff. Dark, Latin-American style. Fads and fancies along those lines. Some go for good looks. Y'know . . . film-star profiles. That sort of thing. Figures. Bulging muscles and all that jazz. Even bottoms. Americans. Ever notice Americans? Young Americans? Tight little bottoms — button-bottoms — sticking out behind.'

'With pants to match,' contributed Helen dreamily.

'Sort of Nureyev in reverse.'

'But with you, it's hands?'

'Hands.' Alva smiled at the surface of the chocolate. 'David has beautiful hands. Really beautiful.'

'Long and thin.'

'No . . . not exactly. Strong. Long? Long fingers, I suppose. But spatulate. Very *practical* hands. I think he knows it. Keeps them scrubbed. Manicured. He — y'now — knows how to use them. Some people. The impression is that they don't know what to *do* with their hands. Awkward. Don't know where to put them.'

'I know. I've seen the type. But not David?'

'Not David. Like — y'know, we've just said — Nureyev. When he moved his hands, it's almost like a ballet. He always knows *just* how to use them. Just where to put them.'

'So,' smiled Helen, 'You fell in love with his hands?'

'And the rest of him.'

'Of course.' Helen tipped her head forward slightly and tasted the chocolate. 'With me it was more basic. With me, I think it was his legs.'

Alva giggled.

'What's so funny about legs?' asked Helen with mock outrage.

'That detective chief superintendents *have* legs.'

'They don't move around on wheels.'

'Sorry. I'm being rude.'

150

'No . . . I know what you mean.' Helen's smile was broad and friendly. 'But he *has*. I speak from personal knowledge.'

'Naturally.'

'Super legs.' Helen's eyes seemed to glaze a little as she gazed into the past. 'At the public baths. Derby Road Baths. Blackpool of all places. I noticed his legs. Shapely. Y'now . . . shapely. A lot of *women* would have been proud . . . Not effeminate. Not that. But good and strong and rounded. And the hairs were like down. Down on a baby's head. Wonderful legs.' She choked a little and whispered, 'A wonderful man.'

'Hey, easy,' warned Alva gently.

'A wonderful week.' Helen's voice strengthened. 'Every day. We saw each other every day for the rest of the week. All day, every day. We were staying only two streets away from each other. Morning, afternoon, evening. He was a detective constable in those days. Not much money, but things were cheaper. We went Dutch. I remember. He was cross because I insisted. It was the only way, though. He wanted to, but he couldn't *afford*. We went Dutch and we went everywhere. The Tower. The Winter Gardens. The piers, the shows, swimming, dancing, walking on the sands. Along the prom. Hand-in-hand. It didn't rain. Not once. Not one drop of rain all week. And when we left — he lived in Coventry, I lived in Huddersfield — we both knew. We hadn't said anything. Nothing specific. We hadn't even *done* anything. Y'know. Just held each other. Kissed a couple of times. That's all. But we both knew. Nobody else. Nobody else . . . ever!'

The tears beat her. They slipped from each eye-corner and ran down the sides of her face.

'Now, there's stupid for you.' Alva moved into her native Welsh phraseology, as she placed the beaker on a side table and plucked a tissue from its box. As she dabbed the moisture from the older woman's face, she crooned, 'It was a silly game. Grown women. We should have known better.'

'No!' Helen caught Alva's wrist, turned her head and pleaded to be understood. 'It's not that. It's — it's other things. Things you'll never understand. Things I hope you will *never* understand.'

'I'm not a fool,' said Alva softly.

'No, I don't mean you . . .'

'Just us two.' Alva tossed the tissue into a waste-basket. 'I know *just* what you're trying to say, pet.'

'That he's a man,' breathed Helen.

'It's not yet a crime.'

'That he has . . . feelings. Emotions.'

'They all do. They wouldn't be complete men, else.'

'That I can't even be a complete *wife*. That if he found somebody else, I couldn't . . .'

'You damn-well *could*!' Quite suddenly, Alva seemed to become impatient with the older woman. It may have been a trick — a piece of deliberate play-acting — because, although younger in years, she was much older in wisdom. Very sternly, she gazed into the sad face, and said, 'Now, look you, snap out of it. If you'd died, what then? You could have. What then? If he's half the man you say he is, he wouldn't have "found somebody else". Not that sort. They never do. Some whore, up some old back street? Come on! Don't insult him. He still has *you*. That's the only thing important to him. You think you're the only one with memories? He has them, too. He can match you, memory for memory. Don't forget that.'

Helen stared up at the woman who, until that moment, had been little more than a welcome visitor. Then, as if unable to stop them, her eyes moved to the curve of the iron lung which seemed to tower above her middle.

'And you can forget *that* old dustbin,' said Alva sharply. In a softer, more hesitant tone, she continued, 'My love, there's only *half* of you in there. Not even the *important* half. Look . . .' She paused, then continued in a voice slow, but little more than a mumble, 'That part isn't so important.'

'I know. I've been something of a fool . . .'

'No. I mean *that* part.' Alva nodded at the iron lung. 'The part inside there.' There was another pause, and Helen waited and watched the younger woman's face. Alva murmured, 'There's a lock on this door, pet.'

As Alva fell silent, Helen said, 'Go on.'

'Not to lock you in. You — you personally — you can't lock anybody out. It's — it's for privacy. If needed.'

'For . . . privacy,' breathed Helen.

'If you want to be man and wife. If you think it's so . . .' Alva dried up. A faint blush spread across her face, and she said, 'Oh

God, I wish I'd never started this . . .'

'Please.' Helen put out a hand and touched Alva's arm. 'I'm glad you did. Very glad. It needed to be said. Needed to be explained.'

'It's not important, you know,' said Alva. 'With the husband you've got, it's not *so* important.'

'But — y'know — if it *becomes* important.'

'Drink your chocolate.'

'Yes. Of course. But we're still friends?'

'We're still friends,' smiled Alva.

'Good friends?'

'We'd better be.' The smile widened. 'After the lecture I've delivered, we'd better be very good friends indeed.'

Johnstone was scared out of his wits. He didn't give a damn about Jakeman; didn't even know Jakeman . . . or want to know him. Nor did he give a damn about Ballester. His sole concern was for Chief Superintendent Rupert Johnstone and the possible consequences of the inexcusable conduct of Detective Sergeant Ballester as far as the said Chief Superintendent Rupert Johnstone was concerned.

'A ruptured spleen,' said Flensing flatly. 'He's being operated upon. Blood transfusion. The lot.'

They were in Johnstone's office. Flensing was reporting the Ballester/Jakeman incident because, as divisional officer, Johnstone was required to know these things.

'He ought not to have been left alone with him,' blustered Johnstone. 'Good God, somebody should have known . . .'

'What?' The soft drawl interrupted the outburst.

'That — that Ballester might have . . .'

'Did *you* know?'

Johnstone's eyes popped.

'Because if you *did*,' continued Flensing calmly, 'and you've been keeping it a closely guarded secret, as a personal assessment I'd say you represent nebulosity personified.'

'I — I — *I* didn't know. How was *I* to . . .'

'How was anybody?'

'People should know these things,' gabbled Johnstone.

'People?'

'The men in immediate command. Hoyle, for example. He . . .'

153

'Hoyle's a copper, not a psychiatrist.'

'Nevertheless, he should have had some idea that . . .'

'Don't talk crap!' Something approaching anger rode the words. 'Hoyle didn't make him a detective sergeant. He was here before Hoyle arrived. Dammit, he's worked under *you* longer than he's worked under Hoyle. Years longer.'

'You're — you're shifting the blame,' choked Johnstone.

'Don't be stupid.'

'Yes. That's what you're doing. Shifting the blame. Closing ranks. The C.I.D. You're — you're working round to excuse what Ballester's done. I've seen it happen before. You — you think I don't know. Think I'm a . . .'

'I think you're mad.' All laziness had left the voice. The hooded eyes were open and glinting. 'That's what I think, Johnstone. Mad and as weak as water. Christ only knows who dumped you in that chair, but whoever it was, he did the force a bad turn. No . . .' Flensing cut across whatever Johnstone was going to say before the words were spoken. '"Closing ranks". That's the expression you used. And you're right. I'm going to make damn sure we close ranks. Not to protect Ballester. Ballester can fry in hell for all I care. But I'll make the ranks close, and close tight, against *you*. This one you're *not* going to walk away from. For once in your miserable career you're going to accept responsibility. Every last ounce of it. No medals this time, Johnstone. Your type. You collect the kudos, even when you've done damn-all to deserve it. It's yours, as of right. That's what you believe. Fine. This time you collect the kick up the arse. That's yours of right, too. And this time it's *yours*. Full weight. This time it'll make your teeth rattle.' He raised his hand, touched his forehead with his fingers then, when he continued, the voice was the old sleepy drawl and the eyes had the old slighty-out-of-focus look. 'Damn you, Johnstone. You made me lose my temper. First time in years. I don't like it. I don't like it at all.'

He turned and left the office.

Johnstone sat staring at the closed door. He began to tremble. To shiver, as if the night cold beyond the wall and beyond the window had invaded the office and penetrated to his bones. Had he been asked he would have claimed that it was anger; a fury which racked his whole body, resultant upon being insulted by a fellow-officer. Johnstone was a great one for self-delusion. He had

154

perfected the art of dodging the truth. Not anger. Petulance. The pique of an inadequate man suddenly faced with the possibility — the *certainty* — of having his inadequacy exposed. That, plus fear.

'You bastard!' he breathed. 'You self-satisfied *bastard.*'

Bill Manford lowered the evening newspaper and said, 'Not at the boozer tonight?'

'No.' Edwina Manford kept her eyes glued to the T.V. screen.

'Why?'

'Don't feel like it.'

'Oh!'

'A bit off colour.'

'Oh, aye.'

Manford folded the newspaper and placed it tidely alongside his chair. Prison does things to a man. Tiny things. It teaches him cleanliness and orderliness.

He stood up from the chair and said, 'I'll go for a jar.'

'Where?' Her voice rose fractionally as she voiced the question.

'The Grapes. Where else?'

'Don't . . .' She closed her mouth.

'Don't what?'

'Nothing.'

She concentrated her attention upon the formalised "domestic comedy" and carefully timed canned laughter. Her "window on the world". That was the phrase in current use. But what world? Not *her* world. Not a world *she* recognised. A strip-cartoon world populated by up-dated Li'l Abners. Nobody really hurt. Nobody really frightened. As true to life as a plastic tulip. Neat houses with no mucky corners. Neat clothes with no stains and tears. Neat people who skated happily through impossible situations without using bargee language, and always the happy-ever-after ending.

Christ, who the hell was kidding who? Watched from where *she* sat, it wasn't even funny. Not funny at all. A hook for a husband; longer inside than out; silent and broody; nobody ever knowing what the hell was going on inside that brain of his. A daughter who'd turned out to be a little tart; bunked in the club before she was any age at all; taken out and given some bloody stuff that had poisoned her . . . and God knows what they'd done with the body. And now the pigs sniffing around. Gatling had to

155

go and get himself killed. Gatling of all people. It had to be *Gatling*. Anybody else, and it wouldn't have mattered a toss, but *him!* All the muck being raked to the surface. All the gossip being talked, and the pigs there with their ears pricked.

Make something funny out of that, Mr Television-man. Hang half-an-hour of comical crap on *that* peg.

She heard the door open and close and Manford left the house, and the smarting touched the back of her eyes.

Hoyle replaced the receiver, motioned to the sergeant clerk to take over, then strolled from the Murder Room. He walked along corridors, then up a flight of stairs and ended in the tiny canteen. He fed a coin into the machine, then carried the plastic beaker of hot tea to the table where Flensing was sitting. He lowered himself onto a chair, placed the beaker on the table and took out cigarettes. Flensing accepted one and, when they'd both dipped the ends of their cigarettes into the flame of the lighter, they smoked in silence for a few moments.

Both wise in the ways of major crime enquiries, they recognised this late-evening patch as one of the dull periods. A time of non-activity. Even boredom. They accepted it for what it was. Part of policing; an aspect of law-enforcement rarely touched upon by the fiction-merchants; something every copper knows, learns to live with and even welcomes as a respite from the other extreme where there are too many text-book "priorities" to do other than work to keep the chaos at a minimum.

'The Brum B.R. people,' murmured Hoyle. 'They've just been on the wire. Holmes verifies what Innes told the Met. A card game, some pushing and shoving, Gatling fell and hit his head against the stove.'

Flensing nodded as if not at all surprised.

'Not murder, after all,' sighed Hoyle.

'We still need him up here.'

'Oh, sure. King's on his way down now.'

'People act very foolishly,' observed Flensing, as if voicing the thought aloud. 'Murder. It starts as a suspicious death. The machine gets under way. We end up with a body but no murder . . . and murder but no body.'

'The Manford girl.'

'It has to be looked into. The smell from that direction is too

156

strong to be ignored.'

Hoyle drew on his cigarette, then said, 'And, thanks to Ballester, our main lead isn't available.'

'Yet,' agreed Flensing shortly.

'Johnstone,' murmured Hoyle. 'How did he take it?'

'There be dragons in those parts,' drawled Flensing expressionlessly.

'Oh!'

There was more silence. Hoyle smoked his cigarette and sipped his tea. Flensing smoked his cigarette.

Flensing eyed the pattern on the floor covering as he said, 'Our wives know each other.'

'Uhu.' Hoyle nodded. 'Alva works part-time at the infirmary.'

'You know about my wife?' It was almost a throwaway question.

'Just that she's in hospital.'

'Ask . . . what's her name?'

'Alva.'

'Ask Alva.'

Hoyle watched the other man's face. Perhaps it wasn't quite as expressionless — quite as deadpan — as Flensing thought it was. Perhaps the off-focus eyes weren't quite as tired-looking as he tried to make them. Even the voice. Not *quite* as dreary. Not *quite* as colourless. They were alone in the tiny canteen. Later — before shift-change and during the various meal-breaks — the place would be busy and buzzing with copper-talk. But now . . .

'How do you view them, inspector?' asked Flensing suddenly. His voice was soft. Almost gentle. 'The opposition. How do you view them?'

'As men. Sometimes women.' Hoyle moved his shoulders. 'We do a job. Sometimes easy. Sometimes hard. Always interesting. We're not expected to . . .'

'Aren't we?'

'Sir?'

'Become emotionally involved. That's what you were going to say.'

'Yes.' Hoyle nodded.

Flensing drew deeply on his cigarette, then screwed what was left into the cheap ash-tray.

He droned, 'A smash-and-grab. Nothing much. Not even a

157

professional job. Not even *half*-professional. Three young tearaways with a stolen Triumph. A brick through a window. A few cheap transistors snatched, then away.' He paused, then continued, 'They couldn't even drive the damn car. Couldn't even steer it properly. Onto the pavement and, sideways-on, into a wall. They left the loot and ran. They were never caught.' Again a pause. A longer pause this time. 'They trapped a woman against the wall. Dragged her along between the side of the car and the wall. She'll never walk again. Never stand again. She can't even *breathe* for any length of time without mechanical assistance. They didn't murder her, inspector. It was never a *murder* enquiry.'

'That's . . . bad,' breathed Hoyle.

'A typical British understatement,' drawled Flensing gently. Without a change of tone, without altering his stonewall expression, he continued, 'I am required to take care, inspector. I am required to force myself not to become "emotionally involved". Not quite true, of course. I am required to *hide* my emotional involvement. Which is not quite the same thing.' He stared unseeing at the floor covering for all of five seconds, then ended, 'Gatling is dead. How he died is of no consequence. He was of a breed and he is dead. That suffices. Innes faces a major charge. I must be satisfied with that. Holmes? We must see what we can cook up for Holmes when he arrives. Jakeman? The truth is, I don't give a damn about Ballester. Had he killed Jakeman, I would have been content. Ballester, despite his being a police officer, is of the same breed. Two more would have been out of the way.' The gentle sigh was not quite controlled. 'I carry a grudge, inspector. A personal vendetta. I keep it hidden. I *must* keep it hidden. But that type — that breed — must be swept from the face of the earth. Those three youths — they'll be men now — they might even be fathers. Spawned their own kind. With luck, they'll be included. I'll never know, of course. But it's possible. And if I allowed myself to show mercy to even *one* man. Who knows?' He gave a single, tiny shake of the head. 'I'll not risk it inspector. I'll not risk it . . . just in case.'

The blowers, ploughs and gritters had fought to keep the motorways open. In the main they'd succeeded, but the long, coned-off stretches where a crumbling road surface was being repaired,

158

brought down the speed of all but the crazy drivers. The closed lanes, the switch from one carriageway to the other, the everlasting blinking amber warning lights reflecting their yellow glow on the piled snow. It was one hell of a night for motorway driving, and the occasional flurries of snow slashing in on the dirtied windscreen added one more dimension to the overall hazard.

The motor patrol officer leaned forward, the better to see the road ahead. His colleague relaxed in the seat alongside him, content to let a driver he trusted handle things pending his own spell behind the wheel. In the rear seat King tried to cat-nap but couldn't. This damn enquiry was turning sour and building up into something of a sleep-breaker; that beautiful eight-on-eight-off plan agreed upon between David and himself was already up the spout. Thanks in part to Ballester. Thanks in part to the Hallsworth Hill crowd sitting on the break-in longer than was necessary. Thanks in part to the London mob digging their claws into Innes's hide. Thanks in part to the unearthing of the murder of Elsie Manford. What next, for Christ's sake? What else could happen?

One thing for sure it was going to be some Christmas. Some *Christmas*.

What next?

Well in the main room of The Bunch of Grapes "what next" was being carefully positioned on the launch-pad.

SIX

Quince and the man with the squint in his right eye were enjoying themselves in their own twisted way. They were playing a dangerous game and they knew it, but the knowledge that the target of their taunts might not be as securely pinned by memories of previous laggings as they estimated ∧ might be drawn to ignore possible consequences — merely added spice to their game. The cops would be around, playing long-stop. It was little more than half an hour to closing time and a squad car *always* had an appointment parked outside The Bunch of Grapes at this o'clock. Even on a quiet night like Thursday motorised pigs were on hand to nip trouble in the bud. Great. Use 'em. Every regular knew . . . and that included Manford. Play the game. Pass the aggro down the line. *Dare* the stir-crazy sod to start something.

They talked slightly louder than was necessary, and every customer who cared to listen could hear. Bill Manford could hear. He stood with one arm on the bar-counter and with his back half-turned on his tormentors. His fingers were tight around the body of the pint glass of bitter — the one drink he allowed himself each time he visited the pub — and, although they couldn't see his face, Quince and the squint-eyed man knew their jibes were hitting the target. The muscles at the back of his neck were taut and stiff and, when he lifted the glass to his lips, there was a steady deliberation about the movement which more than hinted at iron control.

'Bit of a lad, Gatling,' opined Quince.

'Oh, aye,' agreed squint-eye with a grin.

'Tended to spread it about a bit.'

'More than a bit, I'd say.'

'Aye. Anybody ready to drop 'em, you might say.'

'Assuming they *wore* 'em,' added squint-eye.

'Well, aye.' Quince chuckled. 'I mean, why bother, when Gatling was around?'

It was a joke. It called for laughter, so they laughed.

'I reckon,' said Quince, 'a man had to keep his eye on his

woman when Gatling was alive.'

'Aye . . . if he could.'

'If he was around,' amplified Quince. 'Couldn't do much if he wasn't around.'

Squint-eye tasted his booze, then nodded, 'Jakeman knows.'

'Lots of things.' Quince nodded.

'Who would and who wouldn't.'

'Aye.'

'Now Jakeman's been nicked. They'll all know.'

'Nowt surer.'

'He'll draw 'em mucky pictures, if they ask.'

'Aye.' Quince chuckled again.

Quince's wife moved along the bar until she was within easy, soft-talking distance of Manford. She straightened the beer mats and re-positioned the ash-trays.

She murmered, 'Don't let 'em get at you, Bill.'

Manford's face remained set and expressionless.

'I reckon,' said Quince thoughtfully, 'I could name one dirty little cow Jakeman'll mention.'

'You could?' Squint-eye sounded interested.

'I hear the cops have already had her in for questioning.'

'Is that a fact?'

'Oh, aye. Me first. Then her. Now Jakeman. The cops . . . very thorough. Up to their armpits in it. That's them.'

'They like it,' agreed squint-eye.

'They *love* it. All the details. How many times. The lot.'

'Easy, Bill,' muttered Quince's wife. She saw the knuckles whiten as he gripped the glass even harder and added, 'He'll suffer tonight. I promise. He's no room to talk.'

'Why?' The question came from the back of his constricted throat and was little more than a whispered snarl. 'What the hell's going on?'

'They're evil buggers. Leave it at that. Don't *let* them.'

'Who then?' asked squint-eye with a leer.

'What's that?' Quince played the game carefully. Teasingly.

'You said you could name one.'

'Oh, aye.' Quince raised his glass and before he drank added, 'It wouldn't do though, would it?'

'What?'

'To tell everybody.' He wiped his mouth with the back of his hand. 'Might cause trouble.'

'What she needs, surely?'

Quince laughed quietly.

Squint-eye said, 'Bouncing from every wall in sight, wouldn't you say?'

'That I'd say,' agreed Quince.

'But you won't say who?'

'Well . . .' Quince paused then, very deliberately, said, 'Let's put it this way. She doesn't often miss *being* here.'

'Oh! You mean *her?*'

Manford brought his glass down onto the surface of the bar-counter. It travelled less than an inch, but the sound it made silenced the whole room. He turned slowly and walked stiff-legged to the table where his two tormentors sat. A tiny nerve beneath his left eye twitched slightly, but other than that his face was without expression or movement. He stopped at the table, bunched his fists and thrust them deep into the pockets of his jacket, as if pinioning them before they became beyond his control. He spoke slowly and harshly and — or so it seemed — from behind clenched teeth.

'Say the name, Quince,' he challenged.

'Oh, hello, Bill.' Quince smiled a false smile. 'I — er — I didn't see you at the bar.'

'Say the name,' repeated Manford.

'Er — what name's that?' asked Quince innocently.

Manford took a long deep dreath, then croaked, 'You'd better be right, bastard.'

'Look, I'm sorry, I don't know . . .'

'I'll find out. I'll get the truth. And if you're lying, I'll be back . . . and I'll cut your bloody tongue out.'

He turned and, still stiff-legged, walked from the room.

From behind the bar Quince's wife snapped, 'You!'

'Who? Me?'

'Yes you. You cross-eyed swine. Out.'

'What?'

'*Out*. You're barred. That's the last drink you'll have in this place.'

'What the hell,' roared Quince. 'Who the hell d'you think . . .'

'And *you,*' rapped Quince's wife contemptuously, 'had better move your idle backside round here. Start pulling pints for a change. *And* hope Bill Manford doesn't unearth too much of what went on while he was inside. Otherwise he just might.'

'Might what?'

'Come back here and tear your dirty throat out, while I stand by and cheer.'

Bobby-talk. In many ways it can be compared with the talk of dedicated jazzmen when they're gathered together off the rostrum; whether Bix or Louis was the best hornman ever to bring a mouthpiece to his lips or whether perhaps, in some magnificent chorus on one never-to-be-forgotten occasion when they were really riding high, Red Nichols, Muggsy Spanier or Wingy Manone momentarily edged into the top spot; Rich and Krupa — which *was* the greatest skin-man of them all; Goodman or Shaw fronting a big swing outfit . . . or maybe when the Duke or the Count nosed a way to the front.

That brand of argument. But with coppers, although the same enthusiasm is there, the subject-matter is far removed from music. With them, it is the great detectives. Cherrill, the greatest "dab-man" of all time. "Nipper" Read, the real-life gang-buster. Joe Mounsey, who tackled the Pennines themselves in order to convict Brady and Hindley. A handful of super-cops around whom no legends need be built, because what they did and how they did it out-paced legend itself.

As the canteen had filled up, Flensing and Hoyle had retired to the privacy of Hoyle's office. They'd been joined by Adamson and, as time dragged a little and they waited for 3 a.m. and the agreed visit to Manford's home, rank was ignored and they sipped lukewarm tea, smoked cigarettes and swapped opinions.

'George Metcalfe,' murmered Hoyle.

Adamson said, 'The old West Riding man?'

'Had *he* been Head of C.I.D. at the time Sutcliffe wouldn't have notched up thirteen killings. Metcalfe had ice in his veins. I knew him slightly — and knew *of* him — and he'd have laughed where Oldfield worried. He wouldn't have been insulted. Or humiliated. He was well beyond either. He was top-dog. Knew it and made damn sure everybody else knew it. No suggestions. No advice. Even Gregory, the chief constable, would have been told to take a walk. Metcalfe would have used the whole force as a personal instrument. Wouldn't have given a damn about public opinion, or how many innocent men he screwed into the ground. He'd have *got* there. What the hell it took. However high the price. He'd have got there years before Oldfield did.'

'Speculation,' murmured Flensing. He drew on his cigarette, then continued, 'We might do well to speculate upon Elsie Manford.'

'Who murdered her?' asked Hoyle idly. 'Gatling or Jakeman?'

'There's a body — the remains of a body — somewhere.'

'In a grave,' suggested Adamson. 'That's what they tried last time.'

'Innes,' said Hoyle. 'According to the Met. He's coughed a suite of furniture, and admitted the grave trick was *his* idea.'

Adamson nodded slowly and said, 'Seems about right. Neither Gatling nor Jakeman could come up with a trick like *that*.'

'You're the man-on-the-beat,' said Flensing.

'An opinion. That's as far as I can go.'

'We'll accept it. So where?'

'Burying or burning,' suggested Hoyle.

'They don't burn very easily.' Flensing sipped tea. 'Too many people have tried. Slow-combustion stoves. Open fires. The percentage of water tends to put out the fire.'

'Okay. Burying.'

'Where?'

Adamson said, 'In North End?'

'Why not?' muttered Flensing. 'Let's check our own doorstep first.'

'The obvious place is the allotments. Where Lumb has his betting shop. Two years ago? It'll be well grown over by now.'

'That's it then.' Flensing nodded. 'Depending upon which direction things go with Manford. What Jakeman has to say for himself when he's fit to be interviewed. We need brawn and a good supply of spades.'

Thus the talk as a counter to the boredom of waiting. Talk of their own force and other forces; of this crime and other, more famous, crimes. Re-hashes and repeats of moments of notoriety; of open secrets only hinted at to an innocent, outside world. Of the Great Train Robbery . . .'

'That alsatian. Not even a *police* dog. But it scared them from the farm.'

'They were on edge, inspector. The villains are *always* on edge.

167

They're in the wrong and they know it. Blocks and starting pistols. They're there, ready to run. It doesn't need much to flush them.'

'True. But if that dog *hadn't* come sniffing after rabbits . . . or whatever it was after.'

'All that money though, eh? Where? Where did it go?'

'Adamson, my innocent friend, a fence doesn't handle millions. Not *millions!* Only an exchequer. That's the only place you can "lose" a few million used Bank of England notes. One of the new "emergent countries". Take your pick. There's enough, and no awkward questions asked.'

'You think . . .'

'A handful of the right people don't "think". They *know*. Even which country. And already that country wishes it had kept its nose clean.'

Of evil men. Truly evil men. Of Frank Mitchell, "The Axe Killer", who escaped from prison was carefully engineered . . .

'That's what they tell me.'

'True.'

'Y'mean . . .'

'He was sprung for a purpose. The purpose didn't materialise and he couldn't be held. He was too dangerous — far too dangerous — to be held indefinitely. He had to be put down . . . and was.'

'And then . . .'

'Thousands of people pass him every day of the week.'

'Christ!'

'Not stolen bikes, old son. Not nicked milk bottles. It was handy. They were building the place. A multi-storey eyesore smack in the middle of the Big City. He's there among the reinforced concrete. Safe. The biggest tombstone in the world.'

Like warriors waiting for the opening moves of a forthcoming battle. Exchanging the folklore of their kind. Flensing knew a little more than Hoyle, and Adamson would remember those few hours for the rest of his life. For Adamson it was an acceptance into the secret committee of a very select club; he'd been a member of that club but now, thanks to the circumstances and the trust of the two other men, he was also a member of the committee. Mostly he listened. Sometimes he asked questions. And every question was answered without hesitation.

At a few minutes to midnight a clerk from the Murder Room tapped on the door and told them that King had arrived in Birmingham, collected Holmes and was already on his way back home.

'Anxious to be in at the kill.' Flensing stretched, covered up a yawn, and said, 'Like all good little policemen. We never learn. The chase is the thing. The kill is a complete anticlimax . . . even when there *is* a kill.' Then, to Adamson, 'Be "mother", my boy. This stuff isn't tea anymore. Even when it's hot it contravenes the Trades Description Act, but *now*.'

Adamson left the office. When he returned, carrying three new beakers of fresh hot tea, the minute hand of the clock on the wall of the office had passed the upright position. It was Friday, December 18th.

The new day brought about a return of the snow; moist stuff this time, which cleared the last of the mist but, with a rising wind and sub-freezing temperatures, drove patroling constables to the shelter of shop doorways or up backstreets to the high, man-made caves of loading-bays at the rear of the supermarkets. This was no door-knob-trying weather. Even the breakers and the thieves wouldn't venture out in this lot. So, the hell with it! The object of the exercise was to stay alive — dry if possible — pending the early-morning shift change. Empty cartons could be stacked and made into a shelter of sorts. Cigarettes and pipes could be fished from inside pockets. Coat collars could be jerked a little higher, and the old hands had long learned the knack of cat-napping in an upright position with their backs against a comparitively dry wall.

The men doing surveillance duty on Manford were becoming tetchy. Detective constables, unlike the two-man motor patrol crews, they had not been chosen because of their mutual compatibility. Normally they knew each other and tolerated each other, but didn't particularly like each other. Nor was either, because of age or length of service, the obvious senior of the other.

'When's the silly sod going home?'

'Why don't you get out and ask him?'

Surveillance, in the comfort of the Cortina, wasn't easy. It was damn near impossible at this time of night and in this weather, without standing out like a sore thumb.

'One of us will have to get out and walk. Tail him on foot.'

'In *this* lot?'

'He'll spot the bloody car. Dammit, there's only *us* on the road.'

'Go ahead. It's your idea.'

'I'm driving the damn thing.'

'That's okay. Move over. *I* can drive.'

First-gear work. Second-gear work. It amounted to little more than kerb-crawling and, despite the weather, the engine was heating up like the clappers. The needle on the oil temperature gauge was slowly creeping towards the danger mark.

'Somebody *has* to get out and walk.'

'Somebody?'

'For Christ's sake!'

'You feel like risking pneumonia, go ahead. Nobody's stopping you.'

'This bloody car'll blow up before long.'

'Who cares? Then we can all go home.'

'You're an awkward sod. Y'know that?'

'Aye. Too bloody awkward to trudge around in this weather.'

They needn't have worried. Manford didn't see them. Manford didn't see *anything*. Not even the streets he was walking along. His was the pointless, soul-destroying plod around some prison exercise yard; no beginning, no end; merely something to do with his feet and legs, while his mind threatened to tear his brain to shreds. He saw nothing. He felt nothing. Drop the temperature to below zero — drop it until it stopped him in his tracks and froze him solid — he'd have been dead before he noticed the cold. Just walk, man. Just go through the motions. No faster, no slower . . . otherwise some damn screw will shout his displeasure, and break in on your thoughts.

And, brother, what thoughts!

Life, buster. Life. That short gap between some medic holding you upside down and slapping your arse, and the moment they dropped you into the dirt. Not long, but sometimes too long. Too long to have to take it, and too much of it to take. Some men . . . Okay, he didn't envy them. Good luck to the creeps; it fell into their laps and they'd be mugs not to pick it up. Money. The only thing that mattered. Not *their* money. Money their fathers and

170

grandfathers had gutted themselves to earn . . . and now *theirs*. Nice lives. Servants, maybe. Good clothes, good food, wads of notes in their wallets and plenty more where that came from. Okay, he'd been lumbered with the wrong mother, the wrong father — who the hell his father *was* — but that went with the luck of the draw. And their women, too. Ladies. Clean and nice smelling. Good mothers, nice families, a sweet and cosy journey all the way. For everybody. No stinking landings, no sloppings-out, no three-in-a-cell caper with everybody's piss mixing in one bucket in a corner and making you want to puke all night. No keys, no locks, no bars. No hot-arsed bitch for a wife, with twisted bastards driving the knife home about what you couldn't control and what you tried to forget . . . or, if not forget, tried not to remember. Those men — the lucky ones — okay, he didn't envy them.

The hell he didn't envy them!

All his life, he'd kidded himself. All his rotten life. Charging a brick wall, kidding himself he wasn't like other men. That he was one of the hard boys. Too hard to be hurt. Ever! Too tough to cry, too tough to scream 'Enough!' And for what? For this? For a reputation not worth a monkey's toss? Quince and that wall-eyed bastard. *They'd* known. *That* for the bloody reputation. Once — in the old days — they wouldn't have had teeth left for less. Hospital jobs, both. They wouldn't have *dared*. But now? Today? What bloody answer had he? What real bloody answer? Cops with their chops slavering waiting to have another go. A wife who figured her fanny was as private as a public car park. Where to go, what to do. What the hell to *do*. How the hell to *change* things.

The lucky guys? Not envying them?

Buster, deep down, every day of his life. Every *minute* of his life . . . and forever.

With King it was a feeling of well-being. A comfortable, satisfied feeling of a job well done. A feeling bordering upon the euphoric.

His had been a career without too many highlights. A good, sensible, conscientious career in which he'd quietly done his best and better than most men. But nothing famous and no trees torn up by the roots. Indeed, and despite reaching the rank of chief inspector, this was his first murder enquiry. At first, he'd been secretly worried. Could he carry it? Had he the basic know-how to pull his weight? That first evening, when he'd tentatively suggested the eight-on-eight-off scheme to David, he'd done so with some trepidation. In effect, to volunteer to hold a major crime together, single-handed, for eight hours at a stretch had seemed a dangerous thing to do. David had been on these things before and, of course, Flensing was always there in the background to guide the general strategy. But to be the on-the-ground commander was no small thing ... and he'd had the temerity to volunteer.

And the near-certain knowledge that Johnstone would be there, at his elbow, disagreeing with everything on principle.

Odd about Johnstone. Johnstone had kept well clear. Very uncharacteristic of the man. Ever since he (King) had arrived at Lessford to take over second in command on the administration side Johnstone had ridden him and, at times, ridden him hard. In a charitable light, a man unsure of himself, therefore a man incapable of delegating responsibility; knowing he wasn't popular and everlastingly afraid that subordinates would sieze any opportunity to conspire against and drop him. God, that must be a terrible way to go through life! No friends. Trusting nobody. Waiting for the axe to swing, and so sure it *would* swing if you relaxed and became human just for a second.

Maybe Flensing had . . .

Odd about Flensing, too. He (King) had the feeling that David wasn't too keen on Flensing. Nothing specific. Nothing said. Just that feeling that can communicate itself between friends. Not that he (King) had had much experience of detective chief superintendents. But what few of the species he'd been in contact with before had been portly, arrogant types, brimming with their own froth and bubble. At least *that* accusation couldn't be levelled at Flensing. A quiet man. Sardonic. Perhaps even *sarcastic*. But a man who counted every cog in the machine, big and small alike, as of equal importance. With Adamson, for example; giving Adamson credit for *knowing*, because Adamson was a very steady copper whose job was there at the grass roots. A nice trait. The sort of attitude that created a good team.

And yet, and yet . . .

Maybe David was right. Maybe there *was* something slightly off-beat about Flensing. No sweat, no panic, no anything. Not

172

even when Ballester dirtied his ticket. Instead, for a moment, a hint of what might have been mistaken for quiet satisfaction. Wrong, of course. A mistaken assessment. No copper could be *satisfied* when a colleague went crazy and put a technically innocent citizen into hospital. Even a man like Jakeman.

The squad-car driver in the front passenger seat half turned, held an opened packet across his shoulder, and said, 'Cigarette, sir?'

'Thanks.' King took one.

'Holmes?' The squad-car man moved the packet slightly.

Holmes looked uncertain; glanced sideways at King.

'Go ahead,' said King.

'Thanks.'

Holmes lifted his handcuffed wrists and fumbled a cigarette clear of the packet. The front passenger lighted two and handed one to his mate, who was pushing the car north along the motorway. King flicked a lighter, held it for Holmes, then lighted his own cigarette.

In a tiny, pleading voice, Holmes said, 'It wasn't murder, sir. Honest. It was a mistake. Ask Solly. Solly Daniels. It was a mistake . . . and we were all scared.'

Flensing glanced at his watch, then said, 'Any news from the men watching Manford?'

Hoyle opened his eyes, blinked, then shook his head. He'd *almost* dropped off, and he wondered whether Flensing's question was a genuine query or merely a means of keeping things moderately alive.

He said, 'Oh — er — no, sir. I don't think so. The men on duty in the Murder Room have firm instructions. To let us know.'

'To let us know *what*?'

'Whether — er . . .' Hoyle rubbed the side of his face. He gave a quick, twisted grin. 'I'm sorry, sir. I was almost away. The surveillance team have instructions to report when Manford arrives home. The men in the Murder Room have instructions to pass the news on to us immediately they receive it.'

It was 2.10 a.m.

'The best laid plans,' murmured Flensing. 'At a guess, a night on the tiles.'

Adamson contributed, 'I'd be surprised, sir.'

'Too pure, you think?'

'Not the type.'

Hoyle said, 'The surveillance team would have let us know.'

'You have a touching faith in surveillance teams, inspector.'

'They know it's important.'

'To us? Or to them?'

'They'd have let us know, sir,' insisted Hoyle.

'We must,' sighed Flensing, 'work on that problematic assumption.' He stood up from the chair and continued, 'Right, gentlemen. If we're going to make complete fools of ourselves at three o'clock, we might as well be *clean*. A quick wash and brush-down, I think. If we aren't clever, we can be the other thing.'

It was 2.18 a.m. The man behind the wheel was a trained motor patrol copper, with enough experience behind him to *know* there was going to be a shunt. He knew there'd be questions asked, therefore, as he played a vehicular fugue on steering wheel, gear-lever, foot-brake and clutch, he took his eyes from the road just long enough to note the time and the fact that the squad car was travelling at fifty-five. He hoped to Christ the dashboard instruments had been checked within the last twenty-four hours, otherwise some smart-arsed solicitor would have a hair-line crack into which he might be able to insert a lever of doubt and (as always) shove the blame onto the police.

Even without the snow and slush nothing short of a miracle could have prevented the accident; the weather conditions merely ruled out even the possibility of miracles.

It was one of those stretches of the M1 with a steady, prolonged climb; a stretch known to the long-distance men and a stretch which, if possible, they take a run at. A stretch notorious for "bunching".

The slow lane was solid with lorries, bumper-to-bumper, grinding their way to the brow of the slope. In the centre lane heavy goods vehicles with lighter loads or more powerful engines overtook their slower-moving counterparts. The overtaking lane was claimed by the few cars abroad at that hour. The squad car was in the outside lane, pushing to draw ahead of the great phalanx of weight. The articulated vehicle was in the centre lane;

174

it was empty and it had an impatient driver behind the wheel. As the squad car drew abreast of its rear, the articulated vehicle swung right, without warning, and moved into the forbidden overtaking lane.

The squad car man touched the foot-brake and, through the steering wheel, felt the first hint of a skid. He blasted his horn, but it was too late. The artic continued to move right, eased the squad car into the piled snow in the centre reservation, and then the front offside wheel of the squad car smashed into the steel barrier and, like a billiard ball from a cushion, the car was thrown back into the side of the artic.

It happened in seconds. It always does. But to those inside the squad car, each of those seconds was an eternity; an eternity filled with the madness of shattering glass, screaming metal, screeching rubber and a world filled with spikes and projections spinning each and every way. The two men in the front were wearing seat-belts. The driver felt the steering wheel twist and crumple in his hands before his head was thrown forward and the bent rim of the steering wheel knocked him unconscious; his right foot was held by the steel of the twisted pedals, and the bones of his ankle went, but he was unconscious before the pain reached his brain. The front passenger knew the drill. As the car mounted the centre reservation, he dropped his head, covered his face with his folded arms and tucked his feet back, against the seat. The waiting seemed to last forever then, when the impact came and the seat-belt held, he seriously thought his bloody back had gone.

In the rear, King gasped, 'Christ!' and it could have been an exclamation of horror or a single-word prayer. Neither he nor Holmes had seat-belts and King was leaning forward, staring between the heads of the two patrol men. He went over into the front at about fifty miles an hour; the tops of his knees smashed into the rear of the front seats as his skull hit first the driving mirror, then the breaking windscreen. He took it, both coming and going; as the car left the barrier and bounced back into the side of the artic, the bodywork of the articulated vehicle hammered his head back through the windscreen and he ended up where he'd started. In the rear of the car. Sprawling — almost sitting — on the seat he'd left . . . but dead.

Holmes did what came naturally. He tried to go while the going was good. As the car mounted the snow he grabbed for the door handle, missed, and the handcuffs became tangled in the handle and the mesh of metal within the belly of the door as the impact with the crash-barrier smashed the upholstery clear of its moorings. Held there, he rolled and tumbled as the car tore itself into a write-off; he was bruised and he suffered some cuts and nasty grazes, but his main injury was to his right hand. God knows how it happened — later men tried, but were incapable of bringing about the same result — but his right hand was wrenched out of the steel loop of the handcuff; there was massive bruising and the skin along the back of the thumb was stripped away, but no bones were broken.

The ambulance and two local motorway patrols arrived at the scene within fifteen minutes. With help, the squad car man from the front passenger seat had dragged the other three occupants from the wrecked car. He was still shaken, but was helping his mate stem the flow of blood from his forehead. Holmes was sitting in the scarlet-stained snow of the central reservation, nursing the shattered head of King in his blood-soaked lap and moaning, 'Please, sir. Don't die, sir. Don't die. Please! They'll say it was my fault. They'll say *I* did it. Please don't die, sir.'

It was closing up to 2.25 a.m. and Flensing was knotting his tie, after brightening himself up with a cold-water wash. The clerk from the Murder Room entered the washroom and hesitated before he spoke.

'Er — excuse me, sir. I'm looking for Chief Inspector Hoyle.'

'He's human.' Flensing kept his gaze on the mirror and continued to arrange the knot to his satisfaction. 'He's attending to the wants of nature.'

'Oh!'

'Is it classified information? Something I shouldn't know about?'

'No, sir.' The clerk looked slightly flustered. Detective chief superintendents — especially *strange* detective chief superintendents — were very big fish, and had to be handled accordingly. 'It's just that . . . Manford. We've just had word. He's arrived home.'

'Good.' Flensing reached his jacket from a nearby peg.

'Should I tell Mr Hoyle, sir. He left instructions . . .'

'I'll tell him, constable.' Flensing threaded his arms through

176

the sleeves of the jacket. 'You've saved *him* telling *me*. Any lurking time-and-motion merchant should be delighted.'

'Oh — er — yes, sir.'

The clerk blinked, then left the washroom, convinced that this bloke Flensing was a few marbles short.

Manford had, indeed, arrived home. Other than that it must be well past midnight he was unaware of the time. Despite the fact that his shoes squelched and left shallow pools where he trod, he was unaware of the fact that he was soaked to the skin; that his hair looked as if he'd just stepped from under a shower; that even his underclothes were wringing wet and like ice to his skin. He moved into the living room and some semblance of life touched his eyes as it registered that the light was still on, and that his wife was curled in an armchair staring at the blank television screen.

By North End standards it was a moderately well-furnished room. The chairs, although not matching, were unbroken and solid enough. There was a sideboard; a massive, mahogany piece, bought cheap at a jumble sale and occupying almost the whole of the length of one wall. Thanks to Manford's own inability to sit and do nothing, the paintwork and the walls were do-it-yourself decorated and testimony to patience almost replacing craftsman-like skill. The room — indeed the whole house — was one most other North End wives would have been happy to call their home.

It was Manford's home. The only real home he'd ever known. The place he'd always remembered in the sweating darkness of cells. Possibly — even *probably* — the basis of a dream which, after the last spell inside, had pushed him into a personal determination to try a new life and commit no more crime.

He came to a halt alongside the sideboard, dropped his chin onto his chest, and shivered as the wet coldness touched his returning feeling.

There was a full two minutes of silence then, in a whispered growl, Manford said, 'The pigs talked to you, today.'

She didn't reply. She didn't move. She continued to stare at the blank T.V. screen.

'What about?' he asked, and his voice was fractionally louder.

Still she didn't reply. She didn't move.

177

'What about?' he repeated.

Still gazing at the dead set, she said, 'Who told you?'

'Quince.'

'Quince is a lying bastard,' she breathed, but didn't move her head.

'Did they?'

'What?'

'Did the coppers talk to . . .'

'I've already said.'

'They all lie. Everybody lies. *You* lie.' The bitterness, the despair and the desperation seemed to fuse into a solid ball and almost choke him. He croaked, 'For once — just for *once* — did the coppers talk to you today?'

She moved her head, then nodded.

There was more silence, as if he needed time to digest the admission, then he said, 'What about?'

'Gatling.'

'Gatling?'

'Gatling's murder.'

'What the hell do *you* know about Gatling's murder?'

'Nothing. Not a thing.'

'Then why?'

'They — they were asking questions.'

'For Christ's sake, they were asking you questions. Why *you*?'

'They thought I might . . .' She stopped talking. Some of the wretchedness touched a hidden pawl of compassion in her mind. She rose from the chair, walked across and touched his arm. 'Look, luv, it isn't important. Gatling's dead. I didn't kill him. I don't *know* who killed him. Just that the bloody coppers . . .'

'That's not what Quince was on about,' he groaned.

'That's all there is . . .'

'Don't *lie*.'

'What else? What else could there be?'

'You and bloody Gatling. While I was inside.'

'That's a . . .'

'You and Quince.'

'Who the hell's been . . .'

'You and *anybody*.'

'You believe that?' The compassion had gone. Only harsh denial remained. 'You believe all that dirty-minded . . .'

'Elsie hinted at it.'

'Elsie?' she stared.

'Not outright. Christ, you're her mother. She couldn't . . .'

'That dirty little cow? That hot-arsed little . . .'

'*Stop it*!'

His balled fist came down like a hammer on the surface of the sideboard. The inch-thick seasoned mahogany split under the power and savagery of the blow. The skin of his third and little fingers burst, and bones in his hand snapped. It was a terrifying exhibition of pent-up fury being suddenly released, and she tried to step back, but was too late. His left hand shot out and the fingers clamped like steel claws around her throat. She knew it was the end, and her eyes widened with fear. She tore at his hand, but it was hopeless and his arm was as rigid as a girder. She could hear, but she hardly recognised his voice; it was low, with the heartbroken quality of a tortured animal close to death. Nor was what he was saying addressed to her. Nor anybody. The words and the tone went with the shattered hand and his own condition of drenched and utter wretchedness.

'All those bloody years. All that waste, locked away with scum. All the filth and shit thrown at me. And you're out here. Not even waiting. Not even trying to wait. Having it off. Anybody. Any bugger who fancied you. And now they laugh at me. Quince. The coppers. They can all laugh at me. Thanks to you. Thanks to the capers *you* thought you could get away with.

'Inside. What the hell do *you* care? Inside those places. Poofters hawking themselves. Hawking their arses to poor sods who'd kick their heads in outside. What the hell do *you* know? I kept clean. Think of that, you dirty bitch. Think of *that*. Locked away like a dog, but I kept clean. For you? Too bloody true . . . for *you*. Who else? And you conning me rotten every minute. Visiting me. Fannying me along. Then coming home and romping around with any bastard. And I kept myself sane by kidding myself. Believing. Not being told. Not listening. Even when . . .' He choked. The grip tightened even more, but it wasn't necessary. She was already dead, and didn't hear the last sobbing, 'You miserable bitch. You foul dirty cow. You don't deserve to live. The hell you do!'

He released his grip at last and she flopped to the floor, as boneless as a rag doll.

Flensing refused to be flustered or hurried, and this meant that the first news of the accident reached Lessford D.H.Q. and from there to North End, before he, Hoyle and Adamson left to interview Manford. From the scene, via radio waves, to the local force headquarters, then along telephone wires. A police car, a serious accident and a fatality. The combination equated with speed, but as always speed did not equate with complete accuracy or full details.

In the Murder Room, Flensing, Hoyle and Adamson, dressed for off, waited and worried.

'Who's dead?' asked Hoyle.

'They didn't say, sir.' The sergeant clerk looked to be on the point of tears. 'Just that the car's a complete write-off and that, according to the ambulance men, one of the occupants has been killed.'

'No verification?' Flensing was grabbing at straws. Like the rest of them, he knew experienced ambulance men could recognise a corpse when they saw one. Nevertheless, he said, 'No medic pronounced life extinct?'

'The first news came from the scene, sir. That's all we have so far.'

'Right.' Flensing turned to Adamson. 'Your personal radio?'

'It's in my locker, sir.'

'Get it.' Adamson turned and hurried away. Flensing continued to the sergeant clerk. 'Get back to them. Find which hospital. Get onto *them*. Use weight — *my* weight if necessary — and keep the line open. As soon as they arrive, as much detail as possible. Specifically who's dead. Then send it out to Adamson.'

'Yes, sir.'

Flensing glanced at Hoyle and said, 'Acceptable odds?'

'Four in one car. One dead.' Hoyle wondered how the hell he'd break the news to King's wife, assuming . . . He sighed and said, 'Four-to-one. Too short for comfort.'

'We may be lucky,' said Flensing slowly. 'It *might* be Holmes.'

A thing only known to experienced police officers. The "feel" of a case moving towards a successful conclusion. Nothing physical; no tingling of the nerves, or goose-flesh of the skin. Indeed, it would be stretching things to describe it as a *mental* thing. Nevertheless, a "feel". Like the middle-distance runner with his rival at his heels who, despite this, knows he has the edge and that the finishing tape is *his*. Like the ring-wise fighter who, despite his opponent's confidence, knows that all he has to do is keep his cool and, in the coming round, that all-important kayo can be delivered. The seasoned sailor who needs no electronic gadgetry to "smell" a forthcoming storm. The newsman whose hunches always guide him towards the *real* headlines. These are parallels and beyond any normal explanation. It is a form of instinct — almost an animal reaction — and it comes only with experience.

Holmes felt it. Despite his worry about the accident, and the possibility of King dead, the "feel" was there. This most elusive of murder hunts was drawing to its close. Manford held a key — with a modicum of luck *the* key — and if the surveillance team were to be believed he was there, inside the house. The light was still burning downstairs. He hadn't yet even gone to bed. Drunk, perhaps. At a guess, at least worse for drink. Either way, with booze inside him that much easier a nut to crack.

The two surveillance detectives had been positioned to cut off any chance of escape should Manford fight or crash his way out of the house. Not that that was likely. Like most North End houses it was back-to-back and one of a terrace row. Just the one door and, short of taking the pane with him, the window offered little opportunity once they were inside.

Flensing led the way. Hoyle was on his right. Adamson was on his left. Adamson had his walkie-talkie clipped to the lapel of his mac. Flensing talked a soft, slow drawl as they moved into action; as if making sure the other two officers knew *exactly* what was happening . . . and why.

'I often wonder where the writers of screenplays dig up their so-called "background information". Make-believe policemen. Hammering on closed doors and bawling "Open up! Police!". Kicking their way inside. They don't even check the damn door's locked. Then they seem surprised when one of them gets a face-ful of fist.' His hand closed on the knob. Firmly. He turned the knob slowly and deliberately. Without pressure the door eased itself open fractionally. 'Like this, for example. Let Manford know we're visiting, when we wish him a cheerful "Good morning". Just one simple, basic check.' He eased the door wide enough to allow his fingers access, then ran a hand gently along

181

the edge and along the top. 'Door-chains. Good security measures. They can even make problems for eager little police-men. Fortunately for us, that's a trick Manford hasn't yet learned. A light in the downstairs room. No light when we open the door. Therefore a hall of some kind. Pokey. Standard pattern for terrace back-to-back. A pokey hall, leading straight to the stairs. Kitchen — scullery — on the left. Main room on the right. Door to main room closed, otherwise we'd see some light. Watch for the stairs. Unlikely, but some clown might be waiting to try a Tarzan dive from above when we get inside. Let him. Don't try to field him. Stand aside then, when he lands on his face, stamp on the back of his neck. No Fairy Snowdrop tactics. Don't tiptoe. Leather can squeak. Flat-footed. Weight slightly upon the heel. As near the wall as possible. Floorboards don't creak as much there.'

They were in the tiny, unlit hall. The wash from a street lamp stopped the gloom from becoming complete darkness.

Flensing breathed, 'I go in first. Any obstreperousness, don't wait. An arm each. Break them both, if necessary.'

Flensing opened the door in a hurry, stepped smartly inside and allowed Hoyle and Adamson to flank him before he said, 'Morning Manford. We'd like to . . .'

They all three stopped, and the tableau remained stationary for a few moments. The three officers, Manford looking at them without emotion — without even interest — and the crumpled form of the woman on the floor.

'Is she dead?' asked Flensing softly. Flatly.

Manford didn't say anything. Didn't move.

Hoyle stepped forward, knelt beside the woman and felt at the bruised throat.

He looked up and said, 'She's dead.'

'Your walkie-talkie, constable.'

'Yes, sir.'

'An ambulance as soon as possible. Do it outside. Tell the other two to take up position in the hall and at the window.'

'Yes, sir.'

Adamson left, closing the door behind him. Hoyle pushed himself to his feet.

'You?' asked Flensing.

Manford neither spoke nor moved.

Hoyle said, 'For God's sake! That hand of yours. What have

you done . . .'

'Never mind the hand, inspector. Answer the question, Manford. Did *you* kill her?'

Hoyle began, 'You're not obliged to say . . .'

'He knows the patter better than you do, Hoyle. He's been listening to it all his miserable life. This one knows the book backwards.'

'Nevertheless, I think we should . . .'

'Don't you Manford?'

Very slowly Manford's lips curled into a bitter half-smile, but still he didn't speak.

'They never change, inspector.' Flensing watched Manford, but spoke to Hoyle. His bitterness matched that of Manford's, but it held a core of harsh triumph. 'This one has had the lot. God only knows how much he's cost the tax-payers. How many laughing-farmers have poked around in his mind, seeking fancy excuses. *Him*. Not the poor devils he's left bleeding in the gutter. They don't count. *She* doesn't count . . . she's well beond being counted. Fine. They've had their chance. More than their chance. Now he's ours, and he'll cause no more trouble. Where he belongs, inspector. Where he's *always* belonged. In a cage. And he'll die there. Don't mourn for him, Hoyle. You don't mourn for dog-dirt when you shift it from the pavement.' He paused. The bitterness left his tone, and his voice returned to the drawling, slightly sardonic norm Hoyle had become used to. 'He's yours, Mr Hoyle. Go through the pre-ordained motions. Use Adamson and the other two as general dogsbodies. Seal off the house and get a call out to the three-ring-circus crowd for photographs and what-have-you. Oh, and — er — the hand. Elastoplast — whatever you think is necessary — before you pop him into cold storage.'

Hoyle could never remember such a Christmas Eve. During the past six days, as each piece of the miserable jigsaw puzzle had fallen into place, his despondency had deepened. It needed less than thirty minutes to Christmas Day, and his head reeled and ached with the burden of indecisions.

'We should have asked her over,' he muttered.

'No.' Alva knew he was talking about King's wife. She suffered for this crazy husband of hers; suffered *with* him. She wouldn't have altered him, but deep down she knew the damn profession he'd chosen would never ride easily upon a man with such a depth of feeling. She said, 'Her sister's with her, David. What else? What could *we* do? What could *we* say?'

'She'd know.' He moved his hands helplessly.

'She already knows. My love, you broke the news to her. You volunteered. It wasn't . . .'

'Who the hell else? He was my friend. *Our* friend.'

'She's aware of that, too.'

'Damn!' Hoyle pushed himself from the armchair, walked to the table holding an array of Christmas drinks and splashed what amounted to a triple whisky into a glass. He sipped it, neat. He almost snarled, 'Flensing. I've never known such a cold-blooded . . .'

'He has his reasons.'

'Has he?' He tasted the whisky again. 'They must be bloody good reasons. Better reasons than I can come up with.'

'I hope so,' she said sombrely. Then, 'Pour me a sherry, my pet.'

As he turned towards the drinks table, he said, 'He unbent a little. Just the once. If he was talking about his wife . . .'

He turned and handed Alva the drink without ending the sentence.

'Chances are he was.' She raised the glass, 'Let's drink, my lovely. A toast that we never face *their* problem. To each other . . . and that we always can.'

The final piece of the puzzle — the piece that closed the case — fell into place on Christmas Day. A skeleton staff on duty at North End D.H.Q. One man — a middle-aged clerk — holding the fort in the Murder Room. The streets still snow-clogged and almost deserted. Late afternoon in Johnstone's office, just the two of them, and Flensing listened without interruption.

She said, 'I could have telephoned, but that might not have convinced you. I had to come. I work in a cafe. I work hard, I think I'm efficient, and this is the only day I'm completely free. I'm sorry if it's inconvenient, but it seemed important.'

She enunciated each word with a certain care. As if she'd once worked hard to eliminate even the sound of her origin, but had still to be watchful in case that sound crept back.

'There isn't much of a train service from London today. I have to return by one of the few evening trains. But it was necessary to see you. I felt I had to explain.

'It was important that I escape the environment. Vital, in fact. I needed money for a new start. I estimated that a hundred pounds was enough. Gatling. You know about Gatling, of course. He had a reputation, but he wasn't very bright. He could be very easily convinced of things. That's all it needed. All I had to do was talk to him. Threaten him. Threaten to tell my father when he came from prison. I had no love for my mother. Even now, I have no love for her. I suppose you'd call it blackmail. It was, in a way. It wasn't done for the wrong reasons, though. Merely as a means of escape. If necessary, I'm prepared to see my doctor. Let him examine me. Certify that I'm still a virgin. If that will help to straighten matters up here.'

For her age she had an abundance of simple wisdom. Without being prissy, she was obviously "respectable". She had quiet, self-assurance which, nevertheless, fell well short of bossiness. The thought crossed Flensing's mind that she was a young woman any responsible parents would have been pleased to have as a daughter.

'Mother. I don't have to tell you what sort of person mother was. She accepted the lie without question. She played disapproval. Over-played it. She was in no position to criticise, and knew I knew it. I think if she'd shown any genuine shock — any sign of hurt I could believe — I'd have admitted to the lie and stayed. As it was, I felt justified. Gatling didn't mind going along with the deception. His kind. It boosted his ego. He embroidered things a little. He mentioned somebody called Jakeman. I don't know what good it did, but he seemed to think it might add weight. The rest . . .' She moved her shoulders. 'I knew North End. Gossip would do the rest. The bigotry. The eagerness to think the worst of people. Gatling's reputation. I had the hundred pounds I needed, and I was free to start a new life.'

In a slightly gentler tone, she continued, 'I haven't told you anything dad doesn't know. He approved. Everything. I told him what I was going to do once when I visited him. He gave the go-ahead. I . . .' For the first time, she hesitated. 'I tried to tell him about mother. How she was behaving. Just a dropped hint. No more. I — I think he loved her. He certainly loves me. So . . .' Again the hesitation, as if seeking the right words. 'If I can do anything. Say anything in his favour. You'll let me know, won't you? I won't tell lies. He wouldn't want me to tell lies. But — y'know — I had to come and put the record straight. Not let the police waste any more time. I'm settled now. A new life. And, despite what he's done, I'd like to help him . . .'

She had a train to catch. Flensing drove her to the station, sat with her in the station buffet and paid for the tea and scones. He even accompanied her onto the platform, found her a comfortable seat and raised a hand in half-salute as the train pulled out on its journey south.

Back at the Murder Room he'd recovered his normal, sardonic drawl.

'Go home,' he said to the solitary clerk. 'Hope they've left you some of the turkey . . . if only the parson's nose.'

'But, sir, what if something comes in?'

'It won't.'

'I mean the Elsie Manford murder. If somebody . . .'

Flensing sighed and said, 'I've just had a very long and very illuminating talk with Elsie Manford . . . and I didn't require the services of a medium.'

On Sunday, January 3rd, Johnstone tried to have the last word on the subject. In the office of Gilliant, the chief constable, he fought to smash the man who'd humiliated him.

Gilliant wore civilian clothes; he wasn't one of the uniform-crazy chiefs and, anyway, it was still part of the new year holiday period. Johnstone, on the other hand, wore the lot — crowns, pips, poached egg, even soft leather gloves — and as he sat on the edge of a chair, across the desk from Gilliant, the late-afternoon sunlight slanted through the window and seemed to catch his finery in a natural spotlight.

Gilliant finished glancing through the report he'd already read carefully in private, dropped it onto the desk and looked up.

'Quite a catalogue of complaints, Mr Johnstone,' he smiled.

'I thought it my duty to bring them to your notice, sir.'

'You don't like him, of course,' observed Gilliant gently.

'I don't approve of his ways, sir. I don't approve of the manner in which he carries out his duties.'

'Obviously.' Gilliant waited.

Johnstone cleared his throat, then said, 'The conduct of an

investigation into major crime. It should be based upon something much more substantial than rumour and tittle-tattle. It should be based upon facts.'

'Not murder, of course. Not at first.'

'Suspected murder, sir. A suspicious death. *That*, at least.'

'But, for safety's sake, *treated* as murder.'

'In his way.'

'What other way had you in mind?'

'Making enquiries. Standard procedure.'

'Asking questions in other words?'

'Quite.'

'Then testing the truth of those questions?'

'Exactly.'

'As I read it, that's exactly what was done.' Gilliant raised an eyebrow fractionally. 'The answers were — as you say — North End gossip. But they had to be established as North End gossip before they were discarded.'

'A right way, and a wrong way,' said Johnstone briskly.

'I see.'

'They drove Daniels to suicide. They sent Holmes and Innes on the run. Innes committed theft, obtained a firearm and tried to kill somebody in the Metropolitan Police District.'

'You place that responsibility at Flensing's door?'

'I do, sir. And more.'

'More?'

'It's there in the report.' Johnstone nodded his head.

'Nevertheless . . .' Gilliant waited.

'Indirectly I blame him for Ballester's unwarranted attack on Jakeman. An absolute outrage.'

'An outrage,' agreed Gilliant. 'Tell me, did Flensing order Ballester to arrest Jakeman?'

'I — er . . .' For the first time, Johnstone felt the sand shift beneath his feet. He steadied himself and said, 'As I understand it, Flensing was going to interview Jakeman later that day.'

'Interview him?'

'Yes, sir.'

'With Ballester?'

'It seems possible.'

'Mr Johnstone,' said Gilliant softly, 'I hope these serious accusations of misconduct of a major crime enquiry are based

187

upon something more substantial than "possibilities".'

'He harassed the dead woman,' said Johnstone and mild desperation was there in his tone.

'Harassed her? Or *questioned* her?'

'*He* might call it "questioning", of course.'

'As I read the file, most of the questions were asked by Detective Chief Inspector Hoyle.'

'As you will see from my report those two officers . . .'

'In the presence of Police Constable Adamson.'

'A mere constable.'

'*I'm* a "mere constable", Johnstone. So are you. We all are.'

'Then — then there's King's death.'

Gilliant stared at Johnstone's face. He left the chief superintendent in no doubt that *that* observation was not even deserving of an answer.

Johnstone took a deep breath, then said, 'Sir, it is my considered opinion that Flensing's handling of this case *caused* Manford to murder his wife.'

'Caused?' The word dropped like a stone down a deep well.

'Manipulated. That he was *responsible* for . . .'

'That's enough!' Gilliant was all chief constable. The authority he carried was there in his voice. 'I don't expect all officers to like every other officer, Johnstone. I wouldn't believe it, if I was told they did. But what I *do* expect — what I *demand* — is some degree of mutual respect. Flensing holds a rank. He holds that rank because I am of the opinion that he deserves that rank. I'm not infallible. I can make mistakes, and I'm prepared to accept a reasonable argument which suggests I have made a mistake. But this . . .' He touched the report submitted by Johnstone. 'This isn't an argument. This contains no more substance than what you've said since you came into this office. It's little more than the whining of a spoiled child. *Not* what I expect from a divisional officer. Not even what I'm prepared to *accept*.'

'You — you . . .' Johnstone moistened dry lips. 'You mean you won't even reprimand him?'

'I might even commend him.'

'In that case . . .' Johnstone's face was pale with indignation and defeat. 'In that case, sir, I feel I must submit my resignation. I can't possibly . . .'

'A wise decision, chief superintendent.' Gilliant stood up. The meeting was at an end. 'I'll expect it on my desk within a week. Now go back to your division. Be advised. Take leave of absence. It might save embarrassment all round.'

The end of the story? Do such stories *have* an ending? Do the ripples and echoes ever cease? There is no "next week's episode" in real life.

Johnstone was ruined and, to his grave, remained convinced that his ruin was brought about by Flensing's mishandling of the case.

Hoyle was disillusioned, but that wasn't a bad thing; it helped to build a hard shell of reality around the private core of idealism which made him what he was.

Manford went to prison for what was likely to be the rest of his life. He didn't complain; it was what he'd come to expect from a society he scorned. He refused to allow his daughter to be called as a witness. In her, he hoped to continue his own life, and hoped it would be a better life.

Flensing? Who knew what Flensing felt? Not satisfaction. He felt no satisfaction at all. Or ever would.

As for North End. Lies and gossip ruled as always. "Charlie Beat" continued to be policed by Adamson . . . and Adamson had just that little bit more experience under his belt.

very bad editing!